STEVEN MOORE

KILLING KOREANA

BOOKS

Vinci Books

vinci-books.com

Published by Vinci Books Ltd in 2025

1

Copyright © Steven Moore 2023

The author has asserted their moral right to be identified as the author of this work in accordance with the Copyright, Designs and Patents Act 1988. This work is a work of fiction. Names, characters, places and incidents are the product of the author's imagination or are used fictitiously. Any resemblance to actual persons, living or dead, places and incidents is entirely coincidental.
All rights reserved. No part of this publication may be copied, reproduced, distributed, stored in any retrieval system, or transmitted in any form or by any means, including photocopying, recording, or other electronic or mechanical methods, nor used as a source for any form of machine learning including AI datasets, without the prior written permission of the publisher.
The publisher and the author have made every effort to obtain permissions for any third party material used in this book and to comply with copyright law. Any queries in this respect should be brought to the attention of the publisher and any omissions will be corrected in future editions.
A CIP catalogue record for this book is available from the British Library.
Paperback ISBN: 9781036706869
The EU GPSR authorised representative is Logos Europe, 9 rue Nicolas Poussion, 17000 La Rochelle, France contact@logoseurope.eu

Printed and bound in Great Britain by Clays Ltd, Elcograf S.p.A.

By Steven Moore

The Hiram Kane Archaeological Thriller Series

The Condor Prophecy
The Tiger Temple
The Feathered Serpent
The Samurai Code
Of Curses and Kings
The Shadow of Kailash
The Oak Island Enigma
Killing Koreana

"When the spiritual soul of a nation is lost, its mortal death will surely follow."

— Steven Moore

Prologue

Sejong the Great, a humble Korean fishing boat named after the legendary Joseon dynasty's King Sejong, chugged beneath Busan Harbour Bridge into the dark, passive waters of Busan Port. Several hundred yards to the west lay a vast series of fishing docks, spread out over half a mile and where most fishing boats unloaded their catch before it was sold off and transported overland to various fish markets in the southern regions of South Korea. Most of it, though, ended up at the nearby Jagalchi Fish Market.

Rather than veer west to those docks, however, the modest fishing boat steamed onwards north, heading instead towards the international ferry port still five hundred yards ahead. Just a hundred yards in front of the small vessel was a huge passenger ferry inbound from Fukuoka, Japan, slowing as it approached the port exactly on schedule.

Several hours earlier, and far out in the Sea of Japan, the man now in control of the *Sejong* had gone to his humble bunk and retrieved from his backpack a small object wrapped in a leather cloth. He'd gone to the wheelhouse and engaged in small talk with the captain, discussing the weather and sea conditions as they made their way to port. The other three crew were busy at their tasks, two below decks managing the catch and repairing nets, and the third on deck tidying and scrubbing and pretending to be busy like all good deckhands should.

The captain stood calmly at the wheel, and equally as calmly, the man now in charge had removed his recently sharpened filleting knife and, stepping close up behind the captain and saying nothing, he swiftly reached his knife arm around the man's head and drew the blade hard across his throat. Blood sprayed out onto the window, the wheel and the controls in the bridge house and, almost too quietly it seemed to the killer's amusement, the captain succumbed, the new man in control easing the slain chief to the floorboards with his strong arms. He then took his pistol from its leather case, a silencer already fitted, and just to make sure, fired two rounds into the back of the already dead man's head.

Without any discernible difference in his heart rate, the new captain stepped out of the wheelhouse and went to the back of the boat, concealing his weapons on the way.

"Tae-won," he called out to the deckhand. "Tae-won, come here," he said in English, smiling at the young man.

Dutifully, Tae-won dropped the mop he'd been leaning on and hustled up the stairs to the upper level, where he turned the corner and ran straight into the new captain's deadly blade, which he thrust to its hilt in Tae-won's gut. As he had with the former captain, the new man in charge spun Tae-won around and fired two slugs into his skull.

He dragged Tae-won's body to the top of the stairs that led below decks and called out, "Help. Help!"

Kyung, the boatswain, immediately dropped his crate of fish and bounded up the stairs, his long legs making light work of the dozen or so steps. Before he had reached the top, however, the first of two precisely placed bullets entered his skull, the second of which exited from the front, taking with it most of the boatswain's face and scalp.

Not waiting a second, the new captain deftly reloaded the gun and scrambled down over Kyung's sprawled body and leapt into the cargo hold. First Mate Il-sung found himself facing the business end of the man's gun and cowered back against the wall, unsure what was happening but clearly fearing for his life. He didn't have to fear for long as the new chief surged forwards and smashed Il-sung's head with the butt of the pistol and as he slumped unconscious to the ground, the new captain flipped him over, and like the others, he fired two rounds into the back of his head from point blank range.

Ten minutes later, all three of the crew were face down atop their impressive oceanic haul, blood streaming from their wounds and, mixing with the stench of dead fish and squid, the new chief hustled back above decks to breathe of the crisp night air. The entire crew, including the captain, had been dispatched in less than fifteen minutes, and with the first half of his mission complete, the new chief glanced down at the slain captain and sneered.

No hard feelings, he thought and grinned as he continued on his course towards the ferry terminal now less than a couple of hours away.

A flash of blue light caught his eye and he looked right. A boat from the National Coast Guard was approaching fast from the east. He had expected this. It was part of the plan and so far, everything was proceeding like clockwork. He pushed forward on the throttle and accelerated, now angling the boat around the side of the slow-moving passenger ferry and directly towards the port.

As expected, the coast guard boat accelerated too and cut across the bow of the fishing boat, which was now cruising at its full speed, a little shy of fifteen knots. The coast guard boat stayed a safe distance from the now charging fishing boat, trying to ascertain what the hell was going on and attempting to guide it away from the ferry and prevent it getting to the terminal.

The pseudo captain grinned and kept his eyes fixed ahead.

It is almost time, he mused, mentally preparing himself for what was soon to transpire.

"This is the Korean Coast Guard," came a voice through a loudspeaker from the coast guard vessel, the words spoken in the official's native Korean. "We demand you cease your progress and cut your engines now. Failure to do so might result in the destruction of your vessel."

The Japanese man steering the fishing boat didn't understand the Korean words but wouldn't have paid any heed if he could. He was on a course that he would not falter from under any circumstances. Even if they destroyed the boat, it wouldn't change the desired result, and in fact would only speed up the process already set in motion.

"Cut your engines now or we will fire upon your vessel."

Again, the Japanese man ignored the words and narrowed his focus on the easternmost dock of the official ferry terminal. As he pulled alongside the huge ferry, he glanced up. His boat was just a blip in the harbour compared to the towering behemoth that was about to enter the terminal; a baby duck next to a blue whale.

Just then a second coast guard boat roared up on the inside, now between the ferry and the fishing boat. The pilot glanced out of his left window and saw several men clad in military-style clothes bracing themselves along the rails, each with a rifle of some kind aimed at him in the wheelhouse.

"Kanzen," he said in his native tongue. *Perfect.*

He glanced at his watch, and then ducked down below the level of the wheelhouse's windows and knelt at the device that had sat at his feet for the last hour, since he'd dispatched the crew. He had stowed it aboard the vessel in secret before it had set out from the docks at Jagalchi three days earlier. He had served under the slain captain on this fishing crew for the last month and had gained his and the rest of the crew's trust as a hard-working deckhand.

He pressed a series of small switches and nodded in satisfaction as one after the other, a row of green lights flickered in the darkness.

Two minutes.

He stood up again and, with the boat's steering column now locked in place, on course for the terminal, he stepped out of the wheelhouse and edged to the railings. He raised his arms and waved in a frantic manner.

One minute.

"Mian mian," he yelled in Korean. *Sorry, sorry.* It was one of a few select words he'd memorised. "Bot-uh mun-je," he added. *Problem with boat.*

"Stop your engines immediately!" demanded the coast guard through the loudspeaker. "You have thirty seconds or we will destroy your vessel."

The Japanese man glanced from one coast guard boat to the other, then glanced at his watch and couldn't help but smile.

Fifteen seconds.

At the railing on the starboard side of the boat, he waved his arm now towards the first coastguard boat for a few seconds, then, with one final glance at his watch, without preamble he inhaled a deep breath and dived over the railings and disappeared beneath the dark surface of the frigid harbour waters. He kicked as hard as his powerful legs would allow and made it thirty yards from the fishing boat, where he surfaced, surely unseen by any coast guards as an enormous *boom!* shook the fishing vessel from within, splitting huge planks of wood as easily as if they were lolly sticks. The glass of the wheelhouse shattered outwards and a fireball the size of a double-decker bus exploded upwards into the night sky, casting an ethereal glow across the water.

In less than twenty seconds the hull of the boat had split in two and the two separate sections of the stricken vessel now bobbed gently in the slight swell of the harbour waters as the two coast guard boats closed in, their water cannon operators trying desperately to douse the flames with their powerful jets.

It was all to no avail, and less than a minute later, both sections of the fishing boat, complete with the dead crew members and their captain, were sinking slowly to the bottom of the harbour, the surface water settling back to its previous calm.

Now a hundred and fifty yards away, the Japanese man was closing in on the craggy shoreline to the eastern edge of the harbour. The gelid water had numbed his extremities but he was still strong enough to scramble up the small but jagged stone cliff and into the copse of trees that lined the deserted harbour edge. A moment later, a nondescript family car cruised to a stop beside him and the door swung open. He ripped off his sodden clothes and dressed fast in the dry clothing provided on the passenger seat, and with a last glance back towards the harbour he spotted the two coast guard boats, their blue lights flashing, now drifting, aimless, their occupants no doubt bewildered and in shock about what they'd just witnessed.

He then shifted his gaze to the ferry terminal a little further north and inhaled a satisfied breath as the passenger ferry from Fukuoka docked safely and right on time. He couldn't stifle the chuckle that escaped from his numbed lips as he climbed into the car and closed the door.

"Oku yatta, kyōdai," said the driver as he pulled away. *Well done, brother.*

Chapter One

A rapidly disappearing sun from a pastel-hued sky meant it was almost dusk when they boarded the ferry from Japan to Korea.

A biting chill had settled around the busy port of Fukuoka, but Kenji Omaru ignored it. Cold was for wimps. He led his team of three—himself and two scientists—to a quiet area of the ferry, away from nosy do-gooders and returning South Koreans, heading home from shopping or business trips to Fukuoka and beyond.

Fucking Koreans, he thought dispassionately.

He'd never liked them, and was only heading to their country himself for business. The faintest hint of a smile curved his lips.

Special business indeed.

"It's three hours until we reach Busan, Kenji-san," one of his team members informed him in their native Japanese.

Kenji merely nodded. He wasn't one for small talk. There was nothing to say anyway. They all knew the drill. Everything for their 'business trip' was in place. He just needed to secure the team *in country* and set to it. He pulled out his phone and checked a few messages, nodding subconsciously to himself as he scanned his inbox. His own boss had been planning this endeavour for a while now, and it was finally 'go time'.

Kenji felt that same barely perceptible shiver of anticipation he always felt on the eve of a big operation such as this, and as he mentally ran through the procedure in his mind—as he had a dozen times already this day—he knew it would go off without so much as a hitch. They always did. That's why his boss hired him, and why he was paid so well. Kenji Omaru was the very best at what he did.

He glanced over at his two colleagues. His brother, Nanmi, and his sister, Kyota, looked back, expressions void of any discernible emotion . They were the two people he trusted most in the world, and he knew he could rely on them. Comfortable in the knowledge he had the best possible people around him, Kenji allowed himself the luxury of closing his eyes for a few minutes. It was going to be a long night ahead, and a busy few days beyond that.

A couple of hours later, after crossing the Sea of Japan, Kenji headed to the outside walkway on the starboard side of the ferry. He looked down at the dark waters, scanning the surface for any sign of a boat where a small boat shouldn't be. It took him a few moments, but at last he spotted the faint twinkling of lights from the bridge of a small boat that was gradually catching up to the ferry. It was still ten minutes until they were scheduled to reach the terminal.

Kenji checked the time on his mobile phone. He nodded to himself and sent a two-word text message:

: *Everything ready?*

He received an immediate one word reply.

: *Yes!*

Kenji inhaled, keeping his eyes on the small vessel far below that was now pulling up alongside the ferry. He glanced up and saw a set of blue flashing lights approaching, and smirked.

Right on cue.

A couple of minutes later, with the ferry terminal fast approaching as the huge ship lumbered slowly towards it, a second coast guard boat circled in, this time darting between the ferry and the fishing vessel. Kenji heard the coast guards making demands of the fishing vessel's pilot, though Kenji knew the pilot wouldn't respond.

At least not how they want, he mused and grinned without mirth.

Far below, he watched on as the boat's captain stepped out onto the decks and waved his arms in the air.

Nanmi and Kyota had joined Kenji on the starboard walkway and all three looked on with wide eyes as a huge fireball erupted from the fishing boat below, huge sections of the boat cartwheeling into the air as the massive ball of flame lit up the sky above the waters of the harbour.

Ten minutes later, having docked safely, Kenji led his small team of 'scientists' off the ferry. As expected, they passed through immigration with the minimum of fuss. The border patrol section had descended into chaos amid rumours of a bomb blast that had spread like wildfire, the result of which had sent many of the security staff scrambling. Kenji and his team remained calm and polite as they made their way out through the various checks, and his small team was soon greeted at the exit of the ferry terminal building by the other half of their group.

The driver of the SUV, a Japanese colleague stationed in Korea, greeted them without speaking and ushered them into the sleek black vehicle. The driver manoeuvred them out of the terminal and into the heavy early-evening traffic, where they were soon cutting through the colourful streets of west Busan, past the gaudy, neon-rife areas of Daechang-dong and Jung-gu, and headed towards the world famous Jagalchi Fish Market nestled between the thriving districts of Nampo and Jagalchi itself.

Some forty minutes after disembarking the ferry, the SUV carried the team away from the main streets criss-crossing Busan, and entered a more industrial part of the city. Lights flickered on the horizons of infamous Hae-undae and Gwan-galli beaches as night settled over the vibrant city. Kenji recognised the area, having been there twice before in recent months in preparation of this trip. This is what mattered most. This is when the real 'business' could begin, and again he felt that hint of adrenaline start coursing through his veins.

The driver steered them between two large warehouses right on the docks in the southernmost quadrant of Busan. Moments later, just as they approached a large unmarked building, two men stepped out of the shadows caused by the high, sodium vapour floodlights lining the vast yet deserted dock, and pulled open the double doors. The SUV came to a halt beside a shipping container marked with the innocuous words:

Japanese Cultural Mission #4478

Once again, Kenji felt himself smile, though he quickly forced ambiguity into his face. He couldn't let the others see his calmness. They had to remain focused. Had to keep them on point and *mission ready*.

"Welcome, sir," said one of the men, also Japanese.

"Everything is ready?" Kenji asked, though it wasn't really a question. His voice was devoid of any trace of… well, anything. He knew the answer—everything had been ready a long time—asking was a mere formality.

"Yes sir, everything is prepared and ready to engage."

Kenji nodded. He knew this, but still, he wanted to check one last time. "Open the doors."

The man nodded and did as he was commanded. Moving to the shipping container, he first unlatched and then swung open the hefty steel doors, which offered the merest of protests by way of a gentle creaking whine. Kenji stepped inside the large container and approached a single wooden pallet, secured with straps in the centre of the temperature-controlled space. He pulled back a large sheet of cloth covering the contents of the pallet, then took a small step back.

Kenji stared for a long moment at what had lain hidden beneath the cover, imagining the job ahead, his mind drifting beyond the confines of the shipping container and indeed the warehouse, transporting him north of Busan into the mountains in the heart of South Korea. He inhaled deeply, savouring the salty tang of the nearby sea, and the fission of anticipation of the action ahead. He nodded, almost as if to himself, then turned and stepped with purpose out of the container. The man closed the doors behind him.

Kenji looked first to his brother, then to his sister. Neither smiled nor spoke, and instead they merely nodded. Kenji returned their nods, then stepped away.

The leader of the Japanese Cultural Mission then took out his phone and placed a call.

Chapter Two

The old man placed down his fine porcelain tea cup in a calm, practised manner, the way he had thousands of times before.

He sighed slow and deep, mustering a little energy, then rose gingerly off his futon seat by the open hearth, in which a fire had been raging nonstop since he'd first taken a seat by it a couple of hours earlier. This is where he came to ponder and ruminate. Where he plotted and planned. Often, it was where he came to regret.

His ageing joints weren't feeling too stiff at the moment but as winter encroached, dwindling away the riotous colour of a Japanese autumn, he knew he'd soon be struggling with them infinitely more. It was the cold. Merciless and unforgiving on his old bones. Mean and cruel against his thin, papery skin. Gazing at the dancing orange/red flames, he longed for winter to be over once more, before it had even started.

The landline had been ringing uninterrupted for a full two minutes, but the volume was set to its lowest level and the noise didn't bother him. He still hadn't accepted the inevitable technological advancement, and suspected he was the last person in Japan without a mobile phone. Maybe even the world. He was a traditionalist and always would be. He liked old things. How they smelled. The history they exuded. The power they wielded.

Landlines are still essential, he told himself as he stepped over to the antique table upon which it rested. It was how he bugged and checked on the treachery of his former minions and rivals.

After one more deep breath, he slowly picked up the receiver and raised it to his ear. His face remained unflinching as he listened to the speaker's short message, and only the keenest of observers might have noticed the faintest of glints in his rheumy grey eyes. Of course, there was no one else present in his private quarters.

He nodded to himself, almost without realising, as he said, "Very good. Proceed."

He placed down the receiver, almost fumbling it as a cruel reminder that his coordination and cognitive skills were fading, as his eyesight was fading, as were his senses of taste and smell. All the best parts of him were showing their age, but as he made his way slowly over to the huge floor-to-ceiling windows, that in daylight would have afforded the old man an unparalleled view across beautiful Lake Biwa and beyond, he finally let the gravity of the moment light him up, at least on the inside. Then that internal light reached his eyes, widening now even though all he could see through his picture windows were the twinkling of lights from the houses several miles across the dark lake, and the lights of a few fishing boats bobbing a hundred yards off his private shore. He admired the hardy souls out in this cold, but only for a moment. Smart men didn't become lowly fisherman. He admired them, but he didn't pity them. They were weak men, not strong like him. Not survivors.

Not winners.

"Kane," he muttered distractedly, as his expressionless face finally allowed a smile to creep to his thin, dry lips. Slowly then, so slowly it would be imperceptible to the naked eye, that smile twisted into a narrow line of hate.

"Hiram Kane…"

Chapter Three

Kane couldn't help himself. Ahead of him on the trail was the one person that had ever fully captured his heart, and he couldn't take his eyes off her. There had been many wonderful, smart women who had caught his eye and his attention before, but none had possessed that extra something special Kane had found in Alexandria Ridley.

Not only did he find her attractive physically—no, that was underselling it; he though she was sensational to look at. Kane admired her thoughtful mind, her sharp wit, her thirst for adventure, and her philanthropic nature. In short, Kane was smitten with Alex and he still had to pinch himself to believe he could call her his... well, if not exactly his girlfriend, she was someone with whom he shared most things adults in a relationship shared.

All around them, the towering mountains of the Andes soared in all directions. As the head guide of his own trekking company, Kane was in his element guiding groups of tourists along the spectacular valleys and slopes of the Andes, wowing them with his knowledge of the ancient

Inca people and other cultures that had inhabited this terrain for thousands of years.

Just then, emerging from below the cliff line and rising on the thermals, a magnificent Andean Condor soared into view. It never ceased to amaze Kane how those massive birds, an endangered species, with wingspans up to ten feet across, made it look so effortless, while for some of those trekking with him every step could be a struggle, what with the high altitude on many of the primitive trails.

He didn't want Ridley to miss the stunning bird and called out to her.

"Hey, my gorgeous Alex, look, a condor..." he said, pointing to his right.

Almost as if in slow motion, Ridley turned, smiling, and following Kane's arms, she stepped to her left. Except her foot didn't find solid ground and she slipped, her feet scrambling against the dry, dusty earth.

Kane's blood ran cold as he saw the horror on Ridley's face and he yelled "Nnoooooo!" as he sprinted the ten yards to Ridley as she skidded and slid over the edge of the cliff and he dived for her hand and missed and she screamed as she tumbled over the side, her body cartwheeling and her legs and arms crashing into the stony cliff face as she plummeted several hundred feet until her body collided with the valley floor and her destroyed body lay motionless as slicks of dark blood pooled around what was once her head...

"Nnoooooo!!"

Kane sat bolt upright, gasping for breath, sweat pouring from his forehead despite the chill of the room.

He sat there for ages, leaning back on his arms, panting for air after having woken with a jolt from yet another nightmare as he had all too often lately.

It usually took him a few fearful moments to realise it

was just that, a bad dream, and not some horrible reality. At least Kane wasn't drinking anymore. He recovered more quickly from the fears when he wasn't drinking and he was glad he'd stayed on the wagon long enough to have even learned that about himself.

Shrouded in pitch black, Kane stood up from his bed and stretched. In truth, it wasn't really a bed... more of a thin, uncomfortable cot, though he'd become used to it now. He nudged into his slippers nestled beside his bed and, by touch alone, he located the thick robe that hung on the back of his door. He shrugged on the robe in a futile attempt to keep the chill at bay, and then stretched away a knot in his shoulder.

"Not getting any younger," he muttered into the darkness, and would have chuckled if it were funny. It wasn't. Kane was in his mid-forties, though the amount of trauma he'd put his body through, not to mention his mind over the last two decades or so, had him feeling more like a fifty-something ready for the knacker's yard. Despite the chill, he cuffed a bead of sweat from his forehead, induced by his nightmare. The problem with the better sleep he'd been enjoying since he'd laid off the booze was the intensity of his dreaming. Vivid dreams, intense, almost as if he weren't dreaming at all. This time he'd been dreaming of Ridley again, as he glanced at his window, expecting to see the first hint of dawn creeping in through the thin blinds shrouding the inadequate single-pane window to his room. With a deep inhale, he realised dawn was still a few hours away. Pulling the robe a little tighter and deciding to add a pair of socks to go inside the slippers, Kane swung open the unlocked door and stepped outside, breathing deep of the crisp late-autumn mountain air.

He'd been staying at the simple accommodation at

Golgulsa Temple outside Gyeongju, South Korea, for the last few weeks, engaging in a program of meditation, and more importantly, a self-imposed detox after the tribulations that had started in Egypt several months earlier and had sent him hurtling across Cambodia, the U.S. and Canada, ultimately depositing him with an almighty thump in the Scottish Highlands.

Yet, it had gone well here, and Kane was, finally, starting to feel like his old self again. Except the nightmares... horrifying dreams reliving the time he didn't catch Ridley's hand as she slipped towards her death in the mountains of Peru. He had caught her that day, almost certainly saving her life. In the dreams, he missed, always, and he watched on helplessly as Alexandria Ridley's body toppled and tumbled down the rocky cliff, only to be dashed and destroyed on the rocks below.

Even though he had saved her life that day all those years ago, he still felt guilty. The fact it had occurred at all, he had worn around his neck like a penance ever since it had happened, which felt like several lifetimes but was in fact just half a dozen years. He wondered if he'd ever get over it, and despite Ridley telling him the truth often, that he *did* save her life—no one else, only him—it was a truth he was yet to acknowledge.

Kane shook his head as a gust of icy wind buffeted him from over the mountains east of the temple complex. It was going to be a cold day ahead, as they usually were this late in the Korean autumn, and a high moon offered a gentle glow in in the black, cloudless sky.

Kane braced against the burgeoning, bitter cold, but knew it wouldn't diminish his mood and his new-found positivity he'd fought so hard for over these last enlightening weeks at Golgulsa.

The cold, the snow and the great outdoors were calling to him, and he was more than ready to answer.

Kane ducked back inside and hustled into his outdoor clothes... some old combat trousers, a plaid shirt and a thick jumper, and his trusty hiking boots that were half as old as he was. Finally, almost subconsciously, he checked to see if his beloved gold Inca sun disk was where it should be, resting against his chest on the end of an ancient leather strap. The artefact was his most prized possession, a gift from his beloved grandfather, and setting aside his usual reluctance to believe in fate or superstitions and other 'new-age' notions Ridley might have called 'witchy woowah' through a sarcastic smile, Kane always felt better knowing it was there. Tucking it back beneath his shirt, he set off on his now daily hike through the modest mountains, enjoying the thrill of adventure as it began to course through his veins. The terrain was steep in parts, and snow was falling hard. Kane didn't mind. He was a man who embraced challenges, relishing the chance to push himself to his physical limits.

In truth, they were not so much mountains as big hills, at least in this corner of the country. Hiking in Korea was a national obsession. No matter where you lived in the nation, he knew, a navigable mountain trail was never far from your doorstep, such was the natural terrain of the country Kane considered beautiful. Interspersed between the thousands of mountains, towns and cities sprung up like stalagmites, towering apartment blocks in their dozens, reaching skyward and making use of all available ground between the peaks and troughs of the mountains and valleys.

The outdoor lifestyle was one of the things Kane loved about the Republic of Korea—one of many things—and any time he visited he made sure to make the most of the well-marked trails and enjoy the incredible views. There was nothing better, Kane thought, than making it to the summit of one of the many peaks and sharing lunch—or often a bottle of soju—with a group of *ajummas* or *ajoeshis*, the older Korean women and men who still scaled the mountains as energetically as if they were in their twenties, not in their seventies and eighties, as many of them were. Kane had to laugh when he passed Koreans on the trails, which he had once dubbed *The Catwalks of Korea*, based on how fashion-conscious the natives were. They would see him coming along the well-worn paths, wearing nothing more glamorous than normal shorts and a t-shirt, and sometimes even trainers, and they would eye his outfit as if it weren't fit to grace their precious trails. Yet these same people, Koreans of all ages and social stations who judged and scoffed at his outfit, would still share with him their food and drinks, such was the community spirit in Korea's sacred landscapes.

As he surged on, Kane caught sight of various Buddhist temples, pagodas and carvings dotting the rocky landscape as the first suggestion of dawn finally crept in from the east. They were a reminder of the spiritual journey he had been on, and the peace and serenity they offered filled him with a sense of calm that stayed with throughout his hike until, a couple of hours later, Kane returned to the temple where he had started his journey. As he entered, he was greeted by an old friend, who welcomed him warmly.

"Time for breakfast?" his friend asked through an unfiltered smile.

Chapter Four

Heung-min groaned as he opened his eyes a fraction too fast.

Spears of light lanced through the window, its curtain unclosed, and attacked his eyeballs as he immediately regretted the extra round of soju shots he'd knocked back with his friends at the bar last night. It was approaching the end of term—just a few days left—and he knew there would be plenty more revelry to be had before he left the city to return to the temple during the university's winter break.

"Weh-eh?" he grumbled. *Why?*

He hauled himself out of bed and managed to get all the way to the shower before the first ripple of nausea threatened to spill forth. Somehow, he swallowed it back down, the bitter, potent mix of soju and bile making his eyes water. He turned the water to as hot as he could manage and let the not-quite-powerful enough jets do their best to rinse away his hangover, though he knew the acid burning his throat would linger all day.

Cleansed, dried and now dressed, Heung-min grabbed his pile of textbooks from the cluttered desk and dumped them in his backpack. He yawned long and deep as he anticipated another day of pretending to listen to his professors droning on while inwardly imagining his next painting project. Art was his passion, but in a society that still valued academic subjects rather than the creative, he'd reluctantly chosen a history degree. He figured that at some point he'd at least be able to study the history of his beloved arts. Besides, his parents were funding his university tuition, which meant they'd had to approve of his choice.

He allowed himself a moment to appraise his current work-in-progress, an abstract depiction of a friend in her blue work blouse. He'd never show it to her, of course. Only he would recognise her anyway, the series of bold swishes and enigmatic swirls more or less random to any non-trained eyes, he felt certain.

Good. This one's just for me.

With a self-conscious grin, Heung-min grabbed his jacket and pushed the lid down on his travel mug, then shrugged his backpack over his well-defined shoulders, a physical trait he'd inherited from his father. There weren't many other shared traits, something that bothered his father more than himself. Next, he stepped into the small hallway where his shoes awaited him—Korean society all but forbade the wearing of footwear inside one's dwelling. Kicking on his shoes and swinging open the door to his shared apartment, Heung-min opted for the stairs and bustled down the dozen flights before finally stepping out into a cool yet bright Daegu City morning.

"There he is," the driver said to another man in the passenger seat of the van they sat in.

They had been parked across the road from the high-rise apartment block since the early hours of the morning, one of several similar vans that occupied that stretch of road. They had simple instructions, and today it was just another basic deployment, something this pair had undertaken dozens of times in their home nation across the sea.

"Walk in the park," the man responded in their native Japanese. "Okay, let's go."

The driver eased their vehicle out onto the road after letting the target get a couple of minutes ahead on foot. They had already staked out the area from which they were going to strike and it was just around a few corners.

"Be ready," he told his colleadgue, and the two men fell silent as they closed in on their quarry.

Turning right onto the main drag towards his university, and feeling as if he might just have gotten away with last night's drunken activities, Heung-min made his way along the half-mile stretch of quiet road to the KNU, the Kyungpook National University campus. In half an hour the road and footpaths would be streaming with cars, buses and students, swarming like ants on roadkill as they hustled to their various schools and colleges in the education quarter of Daegu. Heung-min liked to go early in an effort to beat those crowds.

It's not that he was trying to avoid people... well, not entirely... but he did want to get a chance to chat with his favourite girl—the oblivious inspiration for his work-in-progress—who had a job at the Ediya coffee shop near the entrance to the campus. He had made it part of his weekday routine, and had managed to overcome his innate shyness to pull it off. More surprising was the fact she seemed to welcome his advances, as timid as they were.

It was thoughts of Han-su that had distracted him enough so he remained oblivious to the unmarked transit van that had been following him since he'd left the apartment block. It was only when it eased up alongside him and two masked men jumped out that he noticed it, yet he was powerless to do anything about the speed with which they grabbed him and yanked a hood over his head and shoved him unceremoniously in the side doors of the van.

Not a single person had noticed.

Chapter Five

Kane eyed Jae-won suspiciously. "How did you know I'd been to the mountains?"

Jae-won grinned. "Because you go every day. And I saw you leave, just after I returned myself. You know, we have a saying here in Korea: He who comes last down the mountain must make breakfast."

"Ah, yes," Kane said, scratching his stubbled chin. "We have a similar saying back in England: He who makes up crappy jokes must do the dishes."

Jae-won shook his head. "Will you join us? We're about to eat." Jae-won knew his old tae-kwon-do protégée would never turn down a meal.

"Thought you'd never ask."

Jae-won led Kane into the warm interior and ushered him to a low table in the centre of the main living area, surrounded by low-slung cushions. Kane grumbled as discreetly as possible. He loved east-Asian culture, but one thing he'd never become used to was sitting on the floor to eat. This was a constant source of amusement to Jae-won, who never tired of seeing his friend's face scrunch up in discomfort as he tried to fold his long legs beneath him, always failing.

"You need to do more yoga." Jae-won's shining eyes betrayed his teasing.

"I'm doing yoga twice a day, every day. That's an hour a day, every day. Because you order me to. I'll never be as flexible as you, mate. You're like some kind of elastic… creature."

Jae-won smiled knowingly. "It is all in the mind, Hiram. Speaking of which…" He paused, appraising his friend. "How are you feeling?"

Kane's lips pursed as he contemplated what seemed on the outside like a simple question. He exhaled. "You know, I think I'm feeling good. Physically, I feel very good." He flexed his biceps and winked. Then he tapped a finger against his temple. "Up here? Still a work in progress with plenty of distance to travel."

Jae-won nodded. "I… I heard you again last night."

It was Kane's turn to nod, which then became a shake of the head. "The dream? Sorry. I just… it's… well, I can't seem to shake the nightmares. It's almost every night now… well, early mornings. I know what you'll say, that I should move on, put the past behind me. It's not that easy." Kane's gaze took him faraway, as if he were looking directly through the walls and seeing something that wasn't there.

"Alex?" Jae-won asked but already knew.

Kane's gaze settled on his friend's. "That obvious huh?" He nodded.

Jae-won had referred to Alexandria Ridley, Kane's long-term, on-off partner, and without doubt, the love of his life. Unfortunately for Kane, the feeling wasn't, if not reciprocal, then at least not acted upon. In fact just a a few months prior Kane had been on the verge of asking Ridley to marry him. He'd been interrupted, and the moment had passed. Kane hadn't seen of heard from Alex since. It was a devastating blow and had set Kane on a self-destructive path over many months, culminating in him almost being killed in Canada. It was the main reason he had come to Korea, to the temple at Golgulsa, to escape the real world, if only for a little while.

Jae-won didn't need to push Kane any further. They had spoken about it enough already over the weeks since Kane had arrived there at Golgulsa, at Jae-won's request.

"I'm going into town today," Jae-won said. "Want to come for the ride?"

"Into Gyeongju? Yes, that'd be great. It's about time I revisited the world's greatest outdoor museum."

In truth, it wasn't just thoughts of Ridley that disrupted his nights. He had learned some things after the mad events of Oak Island before he came to Korea that he was still trying to process, and in fact, was having an almost impossible time doing so.

These revelations weren't especially bad news. In fact, at arms' length they seemed like very good news indeed, and for the world at large. It's just that they had been so shocking, as to undo almost everything he'd ever believed about his good friend and longtime guru and mentor, Professor John O'nians.

It had transpired that not only was John *not* who Kane had always believed he was, but that he was, in fact, very much more. A seismic shift in perception.

Yes, the professor was still a world-renowned art historian and much published scholar on the arts and cultures of the antiquities. That was not in question, and never could be. John was famous around the world for being the leading scholar on the subject, and Kane was fortunate to have studied under him for several years during his time at university.

No, it wasn't that.

Nor was John's position in question as one of the most influential men Kane had ever met. Both as a man, and as an explorer and adventurer. Professor O'nians had taken a young Kane under his wing at the School of World Art Studies and Museology at the University of East Anglia and had guided him through his course and into life with the nurturing and encouraging arms of a favourite uncle who just happened to be a genius. Mentor? That was an understatement. The men had become good friends and had since been on dozens of expeditions together and outside of family, if there was one person Kane trusted above all others, it was the beloved prof.

But what had been revealed to Kane in an old castle overlooking the Sound of Mull in the Scottish Highlands? Well, that changed everything. And not only his perception and understanding of just who Professor John O'nians really was. No, it was much bigger than that.

The old man had offered Kane a job.

Chapter Six

With the final checks of the special equipment needed for their unique business trip completed, Kenji relaxed with his team for a few hours in a small, little-known restaurant deep in the famous Jagalchi Fish Market on one of the many vast docks in the port city of Busan. It was a venue in which high-rolling Japanese visitors hung out and which afforded them some space away from regular Koreans. The Korean owners and those who worked there catered to what the Japanese considered to be their more refined tastes.

There was no love lost between the two nations, evidenced most recently regarding the ongoing disputed chain of tiny islands that sit almost equidistant between the Korean Peninsula and Japan. Known as Dokdo by South Korea, and called Takeshima by the Japanese, the small island chain has long been claimed by both countries as their sovereign territory and to this day they remain a source of aggressive, heated dispute going back more than three centuries.

Kenji grinned. He suspected—in fact he was certain of and indeed relished the idea—that after their 'scientific mission' was complete, international relations might just be that little bit more strained. He didn't care. He had no particular emotional investment in any of that stuff. Politics was for politicians... for idiots. He wasn't in Korea to make friends. He was in the country to work, and his boss paid him to do what he was told to do, and to do it without question. Discretion was Kenji's trademark. That, and his unique set of unrivalled skills.

They ate in relative silence; there was literally no reason for small talk or questions. Kenji's team trusted him implicitly, as he trusted them. The fact they were family only added to that confidence. They all knew their roles, and there was no need to go over the operation again verbally, though Kenji suspected that between now and 'go time', each member of the scientific outfit would be mentally running through it in their minds.

There was no room for error. No margin for mistakes. They had one chance to succeed in their mission, and it was Kenji's job to ensure they were ultimately successful. He had never failed yet. He breathed deep and appraised his team, nodding subtly to himself. *I have no intention of starting now.*

He checked his watch. It was approaching ten pm and they had a drive of at least two hours ahead of them. Kenji knew the route by heart, though he himself wouldn't be driving. He'd memorised every stage of the job and knew the other members of the team had too. He'd checked in with his boss again recently and had been told to proceed as per their schedule. Every single detail of the mission had been planned to the nth degree, and then some.

It was almost time.

Kenji led his brother and sister back down to the warehouse, where they set about loading the equipment from the shipping container into two unmarked transit vans that had been secured for the work. The two men from earlier did the bulk of the loading, aided by Kenji's team as Kenji himself looked on with narrowed, hawk-like eyes and extreme focus. They made short work of the gear transfer and, once secured in the vans, they locked the doors, then loaded themselves into the waiting SUV.

Their team of seven—Kenji himself, Nanmi and Kyota, as well as three drivers and another specialist—set off in the small convoy of two transit vans and the SUV. They left the industrial area of Busan and headed northwest, circumventing the city proper, then bypassing Gimhae International Airport, and were soon in the mountainous region of Gyeong-sang-nam-do Province.

Kenji checked his watch again. Timing was critical, but they were doing fine. If they were a little early, they could simply wait it out in the mountains until the time was right to commence the operation. They all knew the drill and the drivers had driven this route multiple times over the preceding weeks.

Kenji knew their scheduling was perfect. He eased back into his seat and gazed out at the inky blackness beyond the SUV's window, imagining laying his eyes on their prize in just a few short hours.

It wasn't actually his prize, and in fact he cared nothing for it in truth. He cared only about the money he was to collect for yet another job well done. However, if success would mean getting one over the fucking Koreans thrown into the bargain, well that would be a nice little bonus. No one else in the car could see his face, shrouded as it was in darkness. If they could, they would have seen what would have amounted to a rare, genuine grin. He inhaled, and the grin faded into a neutral yet determined expression.

"One hour out, boss," the driver stated from the front. "We're exactly on schedule."

Kenji nodded. "One hour out. Ninety minutes until show time."

Chapter Seven

Kane felt emotionally drained from the constant nightmares that continuously ruined his sleep. It's not that he needed a lot of sleep. He was happy functioning on four to five hours. It's just that he wasn't getting that amount, and what he was managing was fitful and broken.

His body ached too, partly because of the gruelling exercise regime he was on, but mostly due to that irregular, interrupted sleep. He was relishing his morning out with Jae-won. Gyeongju was a small rural city, and had long been dubbed an outdoor museum due to its fantastic collection of Buddhist temples and stupas, ancient burial mounds and other fascinating relics from a series of dynasties dating back thousands of years. A walk around the open-air cultural monuments was just what Kane needed to dust off the cobwebs.

First, coffee. It was only an hour's drive to Gyeongju through the countryside from the temple complex at Golgulsa, and Jae-won had soon parked his car at his favourite coffee place in town, a quaint little cafe-cum-book-store set back across the road from the enigmatic and culturally important Daesong Tomb Park.

The place was already buzzing, despite the early hour, so they waited in line, got two coffees to go, complete with breakfast pastries, and stepped back out into the cool yet bright morning. It wasn't quite winter yet, but in Korea, when winter arrived it came on fast and temperatures plummeted well below zero most days until the locals prayers for the return of spring came to fruition. On Kane's first visit to the country a decade or so earlier it had also been winter and temperatures had reached minus 30°c, minus 45°c if you factored in the wind chill. Kane sometimes felt he had never fully warmed up since then.

They crossed the quiet road and entered one of several main tomb parks, just as the sun made a welcome appearance between two of the massive, grassy burial mounds to their east. It failed to add any warmth to the morning.

"Are you glad you came?" Jae-won had invited Kane to Korea after hearing of his recent troubles, and the latest in a string of near-death experiences.

"To Gyeongju? Of course… you know it's my favourite spot in Korea."

Jae-won looked sideways at Kane, as if to say, *You know what I meant. Answer the real question.* He rolled his eyes. Kane grinned, fully aware of the real question.

"Yes, Master, I am glad I came to Korea." He bowed his head towards his old friend, and it was only half mocking. He respected Jae-won greatly, and genuinely was grateful his old tae-kwon-do instructor had sent him the invite. "I wanted to thank you, actually. It means a lot that you offered me a room at the temple. It's… well, you were always smarter than me. It's just what I needed." Kane stopped and turned to face his friend. "Kam-sa ham-ni-da, chin-gu," he said, taking Jae-won's free hand in his own. *Thank you, my friend.*

The two men continued their circumambulation of the tomb park, making small talk and generally absorbing and relishing the peace and serenity of the area. The famous tombs in Gyeongju, mostly large, grassy mounds with a burial chamber set deep inside, dated back to the Silla dynasty and contained the burial chambers of a series of kings, queens and other royals and dignitaries from a dynasty that ruled from the first century BCE until well into the seventh century. Only a few of the tomb interiors had been made open to public access and Kane had been inside one on a previous visit. On display, alongside the burial suit of King Mich'u, were a series of priceless artefacts, including gold crowns and headdresses, and other spectacular grave goods that would see their owner prosper in the afterlife.

The tombs weren't unlike those found beneath the great pyramids of Egypt in principle, although in construction they were nothing at all alike. While the Great Pyramid of Giza rose hundreds of feet in the air, with a footprint close to 600,000 square feet, the tomb mounds of Gyeongju were humble in comparison. The largest of which, though not small, rose only 80 feet, and perhaps 150 more across its base. They were impressive nonetheless and Kane always loved to visit.

"It still looks a lot like Tellytubby land," he said, knowing full well Jae-won hated the childish reference.

"These are my ancestors, don't forget. I urge you to pay a little respect." Jae-won glared at Kane, yet Kane didn't miss the twinkle of mischief in the older man's eyes.

They moved on from that section of the tomb trail and headed east towards Cheom-song-dae, regarded as the oldest astrological observatory in all of Asia. The modest stone tower, only 40-feet-high, was one of the most famous tourist attractions in the city and already a small crowd of tourists had gathered around it, snapping selfies while, Kane thought, barely even looking at and appreciating the architectural wonder.

"Why don't you call her?" Jae-Won had always been a straight talker but this out-of-the-blue question caught Kane totally off guard.

He didn't answer at first. Not because he didn't want to. He just didn't know how to.

"Call who?" Kane asked.

Jae-won laughed. "You know who. Alexandria. Call Alex, my friend."

Kane frowned at first until a sheepish grin stretched over his face. "You got me. Can't hide anything from you, can I?"

Jae-won shrugged. "So will you call her? It will put us all out of our misery."

Why hadn't he called her? Why hadn't he tried harder to track Alex down? The truth was, she had disappeared. She had watched him leave the Kane estate on what turned out to be an eventually aborted project all those months ago, and he had expected her to be in contact soon after. She hadn't reached out, and all his attempts in those first few weeks had failed to find her. That meant only one thing to Kane: *for whatever reason, she obviously doesn't want to be found...*

"I honestly don't know," Kane said truthfully as they came to a stop in front of the ancient observatory. He gazed up at the beautiful stone work, as if the observatory could offer him some divine insight as to why Ridley had taken off out of his life without warning. The stones remained silent. "I think maybe it's for the best."

Jae-won spun to face Kane. "That is bullshit and you know it. This does not... you don't sound like you, Hiram. What is really going on inside that huge brain of yours? Talk to me."

Kane didn't answer. It wasn't that simple. When everything you love gets taken away... or worse, takes itself away... all that's left is a hole, a void that can't be filled. At least, that's how Kane felt.

Empty. Alone. Helpless. Adrift.

His time at the temple was helping. He was calmer and, almost certainly more important, sober. Drying out. Things were getting brighter in his life and he was making progress. But... without Ridley to share it all with, he sometimes wondered what the point of it all was.

"I'm sorry, Jae-won. I'm fine," Kane lied. "I'll call her soon, I promise. I need to find her number first, if she even has one?"

Jae-won fixed his gaze on Kane, who almost flinched under the sincerity of it. Then his friend's expression relaxed a little. "Now, please confirm something for me, if you would? Are you not Hiram Kane, grandson of none other than Hiram Kane Senior, once a world-famous explorer?"

Kane rolled his eyes, but nodded.

"And are you not also the great-grandson of Patrick Kane, credited with being the brains behind Hiram Bingham's rediscovery of the legendary Machu Picchu?"

Kane remained silent, and swallowed down a little shame. Jae-won continued.

"And are you not indeed the very same Hiram Kane who himself is credited with discovering the long lost-city of

Vilcabamba in Peru, when all before him had failed?" Now Jae-won smiled. These weren't questions. They were historical facts.

"I suppose that yes, I can't deny this... this man you speak of, is me," Kane said, and offered a shrug.

"Well, son, if she has a number, and since you are a very well-known explorer, one suspects if you really wanted to find it, you could. I miss that Hiram Kane, that confident explorer. I miss him greatly." Jae-won slapped Kane on the shoulder. "The world needs the old Kane back. I need my old friend back, too. So unless there's a reason *you* don't want to find her...?"

Kane shook his head.

"... Then I rest my case."

Kane scoffed and turned his head, but only to hide the fact a tear was pooling in the corner of an eye. He cuffed it away on his sleeve.

He didn't say it, but what Kane thought was that if the world needed the old Hiram Kane back, then he would first need Alex Ridley back first.

Chapter Eight

"Come on," Kane said, deftly changing the subject, "let me buy you lunch."

They made their way to Jae-won's favourite galbi restaurant, essentially a grill-your-own-meat barbecue joint. After filling their bellies and warming themselves at the grill, they proceeded on foot into the downtown area of Gyeongju, and soon found themselves at the largest of all the ancient burial tombs in the small provincial city. Not only was this the grandest expression of Silla-era tombs, but it had a more modern story attached, a story that, ever since he'd first heard it, Kane had found both fascinating and horrifyingly morbid in equal measure. He'd never really known how much truth there was in the tale—some claimed it was little more than an urban myth—but as he stood there below the notorious Hanging Tree of Gyeongju, he suspected it was accurate.

Legend had it that during the horrendous Japanese occupation of Korea in the early half of the twentieth century, the Korean women were so traumatised by their treatment at the hands of the military, which consisted of habitual rape, subservience and nothing short of domestic slavery, they often chose to hang themselves rather than face the ignominious abuse of their Japanese overlords. So many chose to end their own lives by hanging from the oak tree that grew high up on the tomb, that under the weight of so many dead bodies—or lost souls, as was believed—the bough had remained fixed in its now downward curved position, unable to bear the weight of so much misery.

Kane couldn't take his eyes off it now, and it was certainly an unnatural position for such a thick branch to have grown. It was almost as if it was reaching out to the ground, perhaps in order to save the lives of those poor women who saw no other option than to use it to end their suffering.

Kane always thought it a tragic tale, and yet he'd never spoken about it with Jae-won, who he knew had lost familial ancestors during the Japanese occupation. He cast his friend a sideward glance. Perhaps it would be okay to ask now.

"Do you think it's true?" Kane asked. "About the tree?"

"The hanging tree?" Jae-won motioned with his eyes and a nod of the head. "Of course it is true. Have you ever seen any other tree that grows like that?"

Kane shook his head *No*. It was returned by Jae-won.

"Yes, I believe it," Kane's old friend confirmed.

Kane had thought as much. The two friends remained silent as they took a seat on a nearby bench. Kane's thoughts turned to Alexandria Ridley and his recurring nightmares. What would Ridley have done if she'd lived at that time, and been forced to submit to the will of such brutal, callous officers?

In fact, that was an unfair question. Ridley was a different breed to most women. She'd proven that on numerous occasions, not least when she'd been kidnapped by a gangster in India several years ago. The man had intended to sell her to human traffickers, but it hadn't ended well for that bastard, who Kane suspected had wished he'd never met Ridley after she'd beaten him to within an inch of his miserable life.

Where are you, Alex? Kane mused.

Jae-won was right; he should track her down, or at least call her. But what would he say if he found her? If he even managed to find a current number? She clearly had her reasons for wanting to disappear. What they were, Kane couldn't know. He was certain he hadn't personally done anything to scare her off. She hadn't even known he was going to propose. Had she? He didn't think so. He'd been careful to keep it a secret. It didn't matter. The moment never arrived. Kane hadn't seen her since.

It was true she had changed after the incident in India and their subsequent escape in Tibet. She'd withdrawn a little, gone back into her shell somewhat, a shell she had to fight to remain out of at the best of times, such was her personality, fiercely independent and in need of nothing from anyone. Kane had hoped to be there for her, to be the one she turned to in her times of need. But she'd made her choice, and for whatever reason, that choice had been to take off.

She didn't even say goodbye…

Kane glanced up at the hanging tree, now being buffeted by a burgeoning late-autumn breeze. An unwanted urge began to creep into Kane's mind, an urge he'd successfully kept buried for the last half-dozen weeks. He wanted a drink.

Almost as if anticipating his mood, Jae-won placed a strong hand on Kane's shoulder. "We should get going," he said. "It is getting cold and these old joints are not as young as they used to be. Come on, let us get back to the complex."

The two friends stood up. Kane exhaled. He closed his eyes for a few moments, in a form of mini meditation, and let his mind clear. Soon, the momentary lapse passed. He turned to Jae-won. "Thank you," he said.

"For what?"

"You know."

Jae-won nodded. "Yes, I know. It's okay, Hiram. I'm here for you. Come on, let's get out of here."

Kane and Jae-won strolled back towards where Jae-won had parked his car. It was only mid-afternoon but the light was already fading and the cold breeze picked up and swirled the fallen leaves in eddies around their feet as they walked. They came to a road and Kane paused for a moment to wait for the traffic lights to change, and turned for a final glance back up at the infamous hanging tree. He inhaled a deep breath. Just then, he heard a screeching of tires and he spun in time to see a sleek black car come roaring around the corner towards them, and with only seconds to react the car mounted the kerb and barrelled directly at Kane and Jae-won, who only because of their instinctive lightning-quick reactions enhanced from decades of tae-kwon-do training were they able to dodge the speeding vehicle that had seemed dead-set on a murderous course right at them.

The two men recovered quickly and stared after the departing car, which then came to a stop some fifty yards up the road. Whoever was driving kept revving the engine hard. Though Kane couldn't see anything through the tinted rear windscreen, he sensed someone was staring right back at him. Then the car screeched off out of sight, and was gone.

"What the hell was that?" Kane hissed to Jae-won, who stared back at him, eyes wide in shock. "That was no accident, was it?"

Jae-won nodded, his shocked expression now replaced by furrowed brows and narrowed eyes. Somehow, the man remained calm. "No... I don't think that was random," he replied quietly. "Not random at all." Jae-won shook his head, letting his gaze linger on Kane a moment before turning and crossing the road.

Kane got the distinct impression that Jae-won had been left wondering who Kane had managed to piss off now, even though nobody even knew he was there in Korea. He inhaled, confusion replacing the shock of nearly being mowed down by a speeding car in sleepy little Gyeongju.

He turned to glance back at the hanging tree a final time, wishing more than ever he was tucked up somewhere safe and secret with Ridley.

"I'm going to find you, Alex," he muttered.

I need to know why. I have to know why you left...

He then turned and followed after Jae-won, jogging to catch up to his friend.

Fifty yards away, standing in the shadowy doorway of a closed store, a man took a phone from his jacket pocket and made a call on speed dial. After a moment the call was answered.

"Yes, it was definitely him," the man said into the phone. "It was Hiram Kane."

A long silence followed.

"Boss?"
"Shake him up."

Chapter Nine

The traffic lights seemed to take an age to change. It didn't matter… it was in keeping with the calm, laidback nature of the city of Gyeongju itself, which oozed peace, tranquility and what some people might call Old World charm. Kane certainly would, and it's what had brought him back to visit every time he'd travelled to Korea.

But the bizarre incident with the car had gotten under Kane's skin just as the bitter temperature had seeped into his weary bones. The heating in his mentor's own car did nothing to counter it, and he shoved his hands under his thighs, which illicited a snort of humour from Jae-won.

"Still not used to it, huh?"

"Get used to this ridiculously cold temperature? Never! I'm not sure how you even handle it."

"Meditation, son, mind over matter," Jae-won said, then cracked a smile.

As the red lights at last turned green, Jae-won eased the vehicle forward east on Taejong-ro towards another of the spectacular architectural highlights, the enigmatic seventh century Donggung Palace with its series of ceremonial bodies of water, known collectively as the Anapji Ponds. The palace was to their left as they passed, and to the right, Kane knew, was the Wolseong nature zone and Gyerim Forest. Kane knew the area looked very much like an archetypal English country scene, complete with towering oak trees and, in summer, grassy meadows full of wildflowers. Now it was smothered in a thin blanket of snow.

Then he spotted it, the same sleek black car that had apparently attempted to plow him and Jae-won down not long ago. A spike of adrenaline sizzled in his fingertips as the car cruised past them on the left. It stuck out a mile among the other vehicles... all white and grey; the colours of doves. Of peace.

"Jae-won, I—"

"Yes, I saw it too. Who are they?"

"I... I don't know."

Jae-won focused on the road, and continued to drive past Donggung Palace and then took a left onto a quieter street, which wound back around the modest-sized temple complex and into the countryside.

As they started to accelerate again, movement in Kane's peripheral vision caught his eye as a black SUV suddenly pulled out from a farm track, tyres screeching as they snagged purchase on the as yet snow-free tarmac.

Jae-won saw too and acted, saying nothing as he accelerated his own vehicle, edging away from the SUV that was now unquestionably in pursuit. He negotiated the weaving country lanes with skill, taking a sharp right turn onto a wider main road and then another immediate left, dissecting barren winter fields that in a few months time, Kane knew, would be full of flourishing swathes of golden rape seed. The SUV followed, its huge engine roaring as

Kane's mind raced, trying to remember the layout of Gyeongju from a birds' eye perspective. It didn't really matter. He had no control of their situation, and was at the mercy of his friend's apparently fantastic driving skills.

"Who knew you could drive like this?" he muttered, to which Jae-won merely grunted, eyes focused on the road ahead.

More importantly, Kane mused, *who the hell are these bastards?* Kane had made an unfortunate habit of upsetting the 'bad guys' all across the world in recent years. Something about being the good guy and doing the right thing really seemed to piss some people off. Yet, of all the places that had happened... Indonesia, Peru and Mexico amongst many others, Korea had yet to present an enemy. At least, he had thought so. Now that was up for serious debate.

He cast a quick sideways glance at Jae-won. The man himself was as pure as the snow that had begun to fall a little heavier, and Kane knew there was no way he had ever made an enemy of anyone.

So who is it, and how the hell do even they know I'm here?

He spun and looked back through the rear windscreen. The SUV was definitely more powerful than Jae-won's regular family car and its driver could easily catch them if they wanted. Yet they seemed content to sit back and engage in a high-speed game of cat and mouse.

The tyres squealed as Jae-won took the next corner hard. Kane noticed his friend's knuckles had blanched white as he clutched the steering wheel hard. Kane braced himself against the dashboard, eyeballing the wing mirror as the black vehicle edged closer out of the swirling snow behind them.

"They're still on us," Kane hissed, his breath fogging the

window as his penchant for stating the obvious reached an all time high.

"Jin-ja-yo?" Jae-won said, sarcasm dripping from each pronounced syllable. *Really?*

The afternoon light was fading swiftly, and the heavy flakes of snow were starting to cling to the roads. Kane was suddenly parched... he wasn't a great passenger at the best of times... and in fact, didn't like cars at all. *This is exactly why I like trains,* he mused inwardly as Jae-won sped around yet another tight curve.

Jae-won nodded then, seemingly to himself, as if to fortify a decision he'd made that he'd also kept to himself.

"What is it?" Kane asked.

"Over there... two o'clock. New friends!"

Kane looked right and saw another black vehicle hurtling towards them along a road that ran at a right angle from theirs. *Shit!*

"They are going to reach the junction before us... I think they are trying to box us in," Jae-won said, downshifting as they approached the junction. Around them, the countryside was opening up, winter fields lying dormant under their fresh winter blankets. There was no way they could leave the road in a regular car.

"Hold tight," Jae-won declared as he shifted up gears again and accelerated hard towards the junction.

"You're not going to make it..."

"We will. Hold on."

There was no time to argue... and Kane clutched his seatbelt tight to his chest, one eye on the black car speeding their way from the right and the other ahead at the crossroads, which thankfully was devoid of any other cars. He understood Jae-won's determination to get through the junction ahead of the other car, and prayed his judgment was as good as his driving ability.

The driver of the other car seemed to understand and sped up too, now hurtling along the narrow country road at what Kane guessed was at least 80-miles-per-hour. It matched what Jae-won was doing, and if they collided, it would be all over for everyone involved.

The junction loomed large ahead, still void of any other vehicles, and Kane's breath caught in his throat as they got within a hundred yards, the other vehicle about the same distance. He glanced in the rearview mirror and saw the SUV had backed off a little, the driver perhaps sensing a crash was imminent.

Fifty yards now. Then twenty.

When both cars were just two car lengths from the junction, Kane knew a crash was inevitable and he closed his eyes and braced for impact, fleetingly realising he was finally about to die after too many near misses.

"Aaaarrrghhhhhhh!" Jae-won yelled as he sailed across the junction, breaking the law and the speedlimit and, Kane realised when their car didn't erupt in a ball of gasoline-fuelled flames and screeching metal after colliding with the other car, they'd made it.

Kane glanced back and to his left and saw the red brake lights of the car as it screeched to a halt. The SUV was still right on their tail.

Other then his scream of adrenaline, Jae-won hadn't as much as flinched, and he surged on, and if Kane wasn't mistaken, the slightest flicker of a smile crinkled his old friend's eyes. He was about to ask, when Jae-won slammed on the brakes, and yanked the wheel hard left onto a barely visible farm track between fields and which only someone with local knowledge would have known even existed. The car skidded through the turn, the backend fishtailing in the increasingly treacherous conditions. The SUV shot past, the driver and his bigger vehicle unable to match Jae-won's sudden move.

They were now on a narrow dirt lane, the snow now sticking to the ground and concealing the ruts and potholes that jarred through Kane's bones. Up ahead he spotted a temple he thought he recognised, Gameun-sa, a little known Buddhist structure off the tourist trail with its distinctive yongmaru ridge-beamed roof, and whose angled eaves cut sharp, silhouetted shapes against the darkening sky. Ancient stone walls lined both sides of the narrow road now, behind which were lines of the tall, spindly pine trees prevalent in the area.

The SUV was still a distance behind them. Now with its lights on, the glare reflected harshly in Jae-won's mirror. Somewhere behind the SUV, Kane felt certain the other black car was trying to catch up. Jae-won maintained his speed, despite the deteriorating visibility and the narrow, bumpy road.

"We can not keep this up forever," Jae-won stated, swerving around another bend and leaving the temple complex behind them.

Kane nodded. "I know, but what else can we do? I have no idea who these people are or what they want. But they seem to be certain who we are. Ot at least, who I am. I'm all out of ideas."

Chapter Ten

The snow was falling in thick swathes now, and Jae-won's windscreen wipers were struggling under the relentless burden. The conditions for driving were no longer just bad. They were actively dangerous, not to mention the fact that two vehicles potentially full of apparent bad guys were following with who knew what level of nefarious intentions on their minds.

Jae-won's wheels battled for purchase against the now slick yet still uneven dirt road, but somehow he managed to keep them on the track.

"We have another growing concern," Kane said, swiping away patches of condensation from the inside of the windowscreen with his sleeve. "The temperature is plummeting." He motioned towards the first hints of ice forming at the edges of the glass. The wipers were leaving greasy arcs smeared across the surface.

Jae-won downshifted the gears, allowing the engine's resistance to help control their speed. Every decision had to be calculated—accelerating too fast would spin them out. Braking too hard would send them into a skid. Behind them, even the SUV seemed to be struggling. Kane assumed its significant extra weight was becoming a liability on the treacherous surface.

"Main road up ahead," Jae-won declared, and Kane was relieved they'd soon be off the potentially lethal country lane.

He spun and looked through the back windscreen, relatively clear of snow and condensation. The SUV had fallen farther back, and he couldn't see the second vehicle but assumed it was somewhere behind the SUV.

The car bumped over a final deep rut, and then they were on a welcome flat main road again, more or less free from traffic due to the awful weather and driving conditions. They passed a digital road sign flashing a temperature that told them it was a bitter -9°C.

"I have a plan," Jae-won declared.

"Good. The road will no longer slow them down," Kane offered, watching their pursuer's headlights dance erratically through what was now almost a wall of white as the SUV also joined the main road. There was no sign of the second car, which concerned Kane…

That concern doubled when he then spotted it as it emerged from the trail into the thick swirling snow behind them.

Suddenly the SUV accelerated and pulled alongside Jae-won's car. Kane caught a glimpse of the driver, blurry through the snow flurries. The driver's window rolled down and for a second Kane half expected the man, who was wearing a hat pulled low and a scarf to his chin, to point a gun at them. Instead, he simply grinned, and pointed at them, as if to ensure thye knew he had seen them and he knew exactly who they were.

Kane was violently thrown across his seat as Jae-won suddenly swerved hard across the road to avoid a small truck that appeared to be loaded with... *are they cabbages?* The truck also swerved, spilling its load of purple winter cabbages across the road, and Kane looked back to see the SUV clattering over the strewn vegetables, and then its wheels must have found a patch of ice because the SUV began to fishtail wildly, before the driver managed to regain control and retake its place right on Jae-won's tail.

"They are very... persistent," Kane muttered, to which Jae-won snorted. It was almost a laugh.

"I have another word for them," he said and shot Kane a sideways glance.

"What was your plan?" Kane asked as they found themselves now in light traffic. Kane remembered it was actually now Friday evening... commuter traffic. It would only get busier.

"Do you remember Bomun Lake?" Jae-won asked.

Kane did, and nodded. "Yes, nice area. What about it?"

Kane braced himself as Jae-won darted in and out of the burgeoning traffic as they got closer to downtown Gyeongju again. After ten minutes of somewhat reckless driving, in which the driver of the SUV seemed happy enough to just stay within view of his quarry, through the swirling snow Kane caught fleeting glimpses of Bomun Lake to his right, its surface dark and choppy in the last few minutes of dusk. The myriad structures of the tourist hotels along its western shore were barely visible, their presence only known due to their garish neon lights already glowing bright against the late winter gloom.

Jae-won's expression was focused yet calm. "Hold tight,"

he said, and suddenly swung right onto the lakeside road between the lake itself and the hotels. Jae-won weaved between cars along the narrow two-lane road, eliciting a series of angry horns as the SUV struggled to maintain the chase.

"There is a service road up ahead," Jae-won stated. "The hotels use it for deliveries. It runs right along the water, next to this road. It is coming up in thirty seconds."

Kane spotted it ahead… a narrow strip of dirt track separated from the lake by only a low metal fence. In seconds Jae-won was angling the car down a shallow access ramp to the narrow dirt track. The SUV followed, and they raced along the lakeside, snow and middy spray combining to create a treacherous surface. On their left, the shrouded mass of the hotels loomed. On their right, nothing but the low fence and the brooding dark water beyond that seemed to Kane to possess a somewhat malevolent quality.

"Up ahead, watch out," Kane stated as a delivery van appeared, backing out from the loading bay of one of the hotels. Jae-won didn't slow. Instead, he accelerated for the narrow gap between the van and the fence. Kane felt himself duck his head, pull his arms in and breathe deep in a futile attempt to make himself smaller as Jae-won's car shot through the gap, sparks flying off the steel fence as it scraped along the right side of the car. The sound made Kane's teeth grind.

It was clear the van driver hadn't seem them coming, and the van continued reversing. Kane looked back just in time to see the SUV slam into the side of the van at high speed. The van was hit so hard that it was tipped over onto its side, and though it was a seriously hefty impact, Kane believed it wasn't enough to have injured the van's driver.

"That's the SUV taken care of," Kane said with little

humour, though it was a definite relief. "Where the hell's that other car?"

"I don't know," Jae-won declared. "But we have to assume they are not far away."

They shot up another access ramp, merging back onto the main road towards the lake's eastern end and joining the busy commuter traffic.

The two friends remained silent for a while, Kane scanning the traffic for any sign of the other black car. They were soon approaching the outskirts of Gyeongju. Hundreds of modern apartment blocks rose ahead of them on both sides of the road, barely visible in the relentless snow storm that if anything had gotten heavier in the last few minutes. Somehow, the main road was free of snow due to the thick traffic, and the going was good. Finally, it seemed as if they were no longer being pursued.

"What do you think?" Kane asked, breaking the silence as the tension at last semed to lift. "Shall we head back to Golgulsa?"

Jae-won exhaled, letting out a deep breath, and visibly relaxing back into his seat. He released one hand from the steering wheel, flexing his fingers after being gripped so tight to the wheel for so long. He then did the same with the other.

"Yes, I think so," he said, turning to look at Kane. "Let us go home… it's been quite a day."

Kane was known for his understatements, but Jae-won had just raised the bar.

"Yes, quite the— Fuck! There!" Kane yelled and pointed across the road to a junction. Waiting to pull out was the other black car, he was sure of it.

"Yes, I see it. Ddong!" he hissed. *Shit!*

Jae-won accelerated as the car pulled out in front of an oncoming truck, eliciting yet another barrage of angry horns.

"What's the plan this time?" Kane asked, sick of the sight of the distinctive black vehicles.

Jae-won didn't answer. Instead, he switched lanes suddenly, cutting off a taxi and ignoring the horn blast. The driver of the pursuing car followed, accelerating to close the gap.

"There!" Kane shouted, pointing to a sign for an underground parking garage across on the other side of the main road. "Can you make it? Maybe we can cause them to crash too!"

Jae-won grunted what might have been assent, and as they approached, and Kane thought they were going to drive straight past, at the last possible moment Jae-won swung the wheel hard right, mounting the curb and shooting through a narrow gap in the traffic, then flew down the slip ramp into the parking garage. The following driver cut across the traffic as well, and as Kane looked back as Jae-won screeched down the slope, he felt sure the black car was not going to make it, and swore as it sailed between two trucks and hit the ramp close behind them, but they were going too fast and the driver clearly misjudged the turn at the bottom of the ramp and there was a horrific screeching of metal on concrete as the driver failed to correct their course in time and smashed bonnet first into a concrete pillar, and came to a stop, the rear of the car in the air, totally wedged between a concrete support pillar and a thick steel fence that prevented them toppling over onto the parking level below.

The car was stuck in such a way that none of its four

doors could be opened, the driver and whoever else might be inside, trapped firmly within.

Jae-won quickly turned around and pulled the car to a stop thirty yards from the other stricken car. Kane watched as he saw the familiar flaring of Jae-won's nostrils, and he immediately sensed his friend was going to leave the car and take his rage to the bastards in the black vehicle.

Kane placed his hand firmly on Jae-won's forearm. "No," he said, keeping his voice as calm as possible, though internally, he felt the same way he thought his friend must be feeling. "I say let's get out of here. Leave them to deal with the police."

Jae-won grunted, but quickly seemed to come to his senses. "Yes… you're right. I just want to know who they are. But you're right… they might be armed and it is not worth the risk."

"Agreed. Honestly, out in the countryside, if they wanted to run us off the road, or shoot at us, they could have. Right?" Jae-won nodded. "The fact they didn't suggests to me that whoever they are, they just wanted to scare us somehow, though I still have no idea who the hell they actually are."

They both looked at the car stuck between the pillar and the fence. Just at that moment, a black boot protruded through the rear windscreen. The men would soon be out.

"Let us go home," Kane said.

"Home," Jae-won agreed, and he accelerated towards the carpark exit. Both men looked at the rear of the bastard's car just as one of the occupants managed to get his head out, and seemed to fix his gaze on Kane.

Kane narrowed his eyes, trying to make out any distinguishing features of the man staring in his direction, but couldn't. He was too faraway. However, one thing gave him a moment of concern, and unbidden, a small knot of anxiety tightened in his guts.

"That guy," Kane muttered as they left the carpark and eased into the traffic heading east towards Golgulsa temple complex. "I... I'm not sure, but... I don't think he was Korean. If I'm not mistaken, the bastard was Japanese."

Chapter Eleven

The Japanese team led by Kenji arrived to within a few hundred yards of the main entrance into Haeinsa Temple, nestled deep in the dark and silent mountains east of the sprawling city of Daegu.

All was still and quiet. There were no settlements of any note within at least ten miles. The two unmarked transit vans pulled onto a deserted farm trail, out of sight from the main road, though at this late hour Kenji considered any through traffic unlikely. Kenji and Kyota pulled lanyards from their pockets and hung them around their necks. The lanyards stated their names, with Romanised lettering, and declared they were with the:

Japanese Cultural Mission #4478
Science of Antiquities Research Team

"Are you ready?" Kenji asked his sister. It was not really a question.

"Yes, sir," she replied, keeping the verbal communications formal and succinct. Kenji retrieved a shiny briefcase from the floor by his feet and rested it on the seat next to him. He then clicked the button and waited as his window slid down a little, enjoying the snap of the cold air as it rushed in around him. After a slow, deep breath and an equally slow exhale, he buzzed the window back up again. The driver looked back at him expectantly.

"Let us all do our duty, and make sure we do it well. We will make no mistakes."

The message was simple, yet everyone nodded their affirmation. A subtle nod told the driver his boss was ready. He eased the SUV back off the farm trail and onto the dark, empty main road and drove steadily east the remaining few hundred yards. The approach was on a slight decline, and Kenji could just make out a few dim lights illuminating the main structure in the middle of the complex. He felt his heart rate tick up just a touch, yet he remained calm and focused.

Through the front window of the SUV he watched as the main entrance gates appeared out of the gloom, barely illuminated by elevated spotlights either side of the steel gates. A fine mist drifted across the road and entrance area, adding an ethereal glow to the environment. A moment later the SUV came to a stop just in front of the gates. Gravel crunched gently beneath the tires. He glanced at Kyota. She nodded.

"Okay," was all he said. The pair of scientists climbed slowly out of the vehicle, just as an armed guard ambled out of the brick security hut twenty feet inside the gates.

"You are late," the approaching security officer said with barely contained disgust. He had been told the Japanese scientists spoke his native Korean language, so he didn't bother to use the basic Japanese all Koreans learned in college.

"Yes, we are sorry. Our ferry was delayed. Please, forgive us," Kenji replied in flawless Korean. He bowed his head, which elicited little more than a shrug from the clearly irritated security man, who looked as if he'd been sleeping less than two minutes ago and who seemed as if he would rather be anywhere else rather than there in the middle of the night. Internally, Kenji smirked.

"Open the gates," the guard called out to his colleague still inside the hut. There was no answer. Sighing, he grabbed the walkie talkie from his belt, which crackled to life. "Dan-mi? Open the gates."

Somewhere inside the hut, Dan-mi jumped as his walkie talkie squawked on the desk upon which his feet were planted. He scrambled for the device. "Do-bu?"

"Open the damn gates. Now!" Do-bu turned to the scientists. "Kids, eh?"

Kenji offered a half smile and shrugged. The fingers of his right hand flexed a little as the electric steel gates started to swing open.

"Bring the vehicle inside. The car park is a hundred yards down this service road," Do-bu said, waving at the road, before he turned and began walking away. "I will follow you and show you to your—"

The first bullet cut off his words as it penetrated his neck and passed right through his throat. His hand flew to the gaping wound as human instinct caused him to turn, exposing his face. As Kyota trotted past Do-bu, Kenji's second bullet obliterated the security man's face and he was dead before his body crumpled to the floor.

Kenji walked calmly towards the hut, but before he got there he heard the deft thud of two muffled shots putting an end to the second security guard. It had all taken no more than a minute.

Only five minutes later, the two transit vans and the SUV were inside the temple complex and the gates were closed and locked behind them. Two of the team had already hauled the dead guards into the back of one of the vans. One team member, the Korean language specialist, had taken his place in the security hut, complete with uniform.

Kenji pulled his phone from his pocket and placed a call.

After just a couple of rings an old man in Japan answered.

"We are in. We are ready to commence," Kenji told him. There followed a long pause. Kenji heard the wheezing breaths of his boss, and he sensed the excitement in the old man.

Finally his boss answered. His words were slow and cold. "Then take it. Take it all, now, and remove their soul."

Chapter Twelve

Such was the cultural importance of the *Tripitaka Koreana*, it was a source of reverence, not only to the Korean nation, but to the Buddhist community around the globe. It remained the most complete version of its kind anywhere in the world, and thus was a unique and priceless artefact to be protected and preserved at all costs.

This meant gaining access to it was difficult, if not impossible. Only three people on the planet knew the code to access the inner sanctum, known in Korean as the Palman Dae-jang-gyeong, in which the 81,258 beautifully carved wooden blocks of the Tripitaka were kept.

The centre's head curator, a Mr Ki-sung Park, was one of those with access. The only other two people with access to the codes were known only to Mr Park himself.

Kenji and his team hadn't been able to locate the curator, just as they had expected. It didn not matter. There was always another way to achieve one's goals. That's why Kenji's brother was here on the team. The former Japanese military recruit was a trained explosives specialist. He wasted no time setting about his task.

As Kenji watched on, Nanmi, who had already retrieved his equipment from the SUV, laid it out on the wooden terrace of the eastern building of the Haeinsa Temple complex. It was a modest collection of four buildings. Two long parallel main structures perhaps a hundred feet long and quarter as wide were closed in at each end by two much smaller buildings, almost completing a large rectangle.

The complex had been custom-built to house the Tripitaka in the fifteenth century, though ironically, it had been destroyed several times in the past by Korea's Japanese invaders, who had long since tried to get their hands on the Tripitaka Koreana after failing repeatedly to construct their own version. The buildings had stood in their current guise, unharmed, since the nineteenth century and remained a beautiful example of traditional Korean Buddhist temple architecture.

None of that mattered to Nanmi as he delicately set a series of small yet powerful percussive devices along the four edges of the high-tech security doors protecting the priceless artefacts within. Nanmi was skilled enough to know that no actual damage would befall the objects inside, which were protected by a second inner wall of security. The small explosions would merely destroy the outer doors, safely and effectively. Still, it didn't mean his heart wasn't racing as he looked to his boss, his brother Kenji, and nodded to inform Kenji his work was done. It was time to blow the doors.

Kenji nodded back. There was no need to thank his brother for doing his duty.

"We should stand back," Nanmi said, "just in case." The group of pseudo-scientists gathered behind the large wooden pillars that formed the outer portico to the complex, and watched on in anticipation as Nanmi clutched a hand-held plastic device that looked like nothing more than a digital car key. "Ready?" he asked.

Kenji nodded. Nanmi inhaled, and with a steady hand, he pressed the small green button on the device. Immediately, a series of deep thuds resounded, like a boxer's glove slamming into a hanging punch bag, one after the other... *dhum—dhum—dhum—dhum—dhum—dhum— dhum—dhum—* until all fell silent and eight thin columns of smoke appeared and then swirled into the air, dissipating into the night sky in seconds.

Nanmi rushed over to the doors, ready to support them if they fell outwards. They didn't fall, but he called to the two other men with them to help him lower them to the ground. Kenji and Kyota watched on as, in under two minutes, the outer ribs protecting the beating heart of the Korean nation were removed, revealing the precious objects within.

Kenji couldn't help but grin as he stepped through the doorway and saw with his own eyes for the first time what it was that his boss apparently coveted so much. There before him stood row after row of ornate shelving units, each containing hundreds of the priceless carved blocks that formed the Tripitaka. Carved over an eleven-year period between 1237 and 1248, the *Tripitaka Koreana* was considered the most complete collection of Buddhist texts, laws and treaties in existence, and were created as an idealistic appeal to the authority of the Buddha in the defence of Korea against the Mongol invasions.

Kenji inhaled. *In defence? How did that work out for you?* he mused.

The Tripitaka Hall smelled ancient, of wood and dust,

and practically reeked of history and... *What is that other subtle aroma... destiny?* He literally could not give a shit.

He turned and looked at each of his team members in turn. All nodded. They were ready. "Get to it."

Each of the players knew their roles. They had only two hours to remove several thousand of the unique wooden blocks. It had to be done methodically, to ensure the pieces were not damaged or mixed up in any way. That was a key requirement of their boss and the benefactor of the endeavour. With the transit vans parked close, the team got to work, carefully removing block after block and gently storing them in specially designed padded bags that each held twenty of the carved blocks. They were then transferred to the vans, and stacked neatly within.

Only one of the team didn't join in the theft. Instead, Nanmi busied himself setting dozens more of the concussive explosive devices. This time, however, they weren't set to merely open the doors. Once he was finished, he would have set enough of the devices, placed strategically around the entire inside of the Tripitaka Hall, that upon one single click of the button on the device he carried, the entire cultural masterpiece could be destroyed and every single remaining carved block reduced to ashes.

It was an excellent backup security plan.

With one simple command, and one even simpler click of a button, the beating heart and soul of a nation would be dead.

Chapter Thirteen

Just two hours after blowing off the doors of the Tripitaka Hall, Kenji and his team had carefully removed close to 4,000 of the priceless carved tablets. It was approximately five percent of the entire collection. Enough to have rendered it destroyed.

It was akin to removing a human heart... a body simply couldn't survive without it.

The night had chilled further and Kenji wondered if snow might even be imminent as the last of the custom-made block carriers was loaded into the transits. After repositioning the doors to the main hall as best as they could—a small act of civility Nanmi insisted upon, to which Kenji had barely shrugged—the team clambered back into the vehicles and headed out of the Haeinsa temple complex and off into the quiet pre-dawn darkness.

In the small hours of the morning the country roads remained deserted, though it was only an hour until they arrived on the outskirts of Daegu, Korea's third largest city and, Kenji thought, a city with next to no distinguishing features. He had of course visited before in order to source the location of the next stage of their operation. The drivers of the convoy all knew the location too and he trusted them to recall the route without the need for GPS, which might, at a later date, somehow betray their involvement.

He relaxed back into his seat, gazing abstractly through his window as tower after tower of apartment buildings, some run down and dating from the seventies and eighties, others angular, sparkling new edifices, flashed by. The road traffic was picking up as early risers made their way to their jobs, and Kenji marvelled as he noticed that every single car on the road was either white, grey or black, ninety percent of which were the Korean brand Kia.

The cars are as dull as the people and the buildings here… total drabbery, he mused, but he didn't smile.

They were getting close to their secure location in downtown Daegu. It was the riskiest part of the operation so far… there was a slim chance of having being seen, so they had to remain vigilant and diligent.

Of course, they would not hesitate to eliminate anyone who posed a risk to the operation. That was just a simple yet fundamental part of the job to Kenji, and he had never lost a moment's sleep after dispatching anyone who needed dispatching. In fact, he kind of enjoyed it. There was a cold, callous streak in him he didn't deny. Some might have called it psychopathic. He didn't care. He killed when he had to. Survival of the fittest, nothing more.

"Almost there, boss," the driver stated. "Five minutes."

Kenji didn't answer. It was almost dawn now and the streets in the Samdeok area of downtown Daegu were busy with commuters as foot traffic bustled along the sidewalks.

He spotted the local district fire station and knew they were getting close.

The convoy—deliberately allowing their vehicles to drift apart so as not to arouse any unwanted attention—veered east past the Novotel Hotel, then slightly west into a back alley towards a series of warehouses, some of which appeared abandoned. One had been leased to a fake Korean business just a month ago. That's where they headed.

A minute later, the driver jumped out and unlocked a set of grimy warehouse doors, then swung them open. He eased the SUV inside, and was quickly followed by first one of the unmarked transits, and a few seconds later, the second drove in. He swung the doors shut and locked them from the inside.

The team wasted no time transferring the stolen Tripitaka blocks to a pair of pallets set within another shipping container. Twenty minutes later, all the blocks were safely stowed on the pallets. Kyota took a series of photos with her camera phone, and then Nanmi locked the blocks inside the container.

Finally, Kenji allowed himself a moment to breathe. It was done. The first and second stages of the project were complete. As he had no doubt it would, it had all gone off without so much as a hint of a hitch. He walked over to the rear of the vast warehouse and ascended a flight of steel steps to the mezzanine floor above. The sound of his boots echoed off the steel around the old concrete and brick building. Once at the top he turned to the left and walked towards what had once been an office. The lights were off and the door was locked. He pulled a key from his pocket and unlocked the door, then casually stepped inside. He flicked on the light.

Behind a door at the back of the old office was a large walk-in closet. That too was locked, but he unlocked it and stepped quietly inside. This time he didn't turn on the light.

In the corner, hunched on the ground in the darkness and chained to a cold, broken radiator, was the shadowy silhouette of a young man. The stricken figure grunted something unintelligible that might have been a plea for water. Kenji didn't care. He stepped over to the cowering form, and after a cruel pause, he unleashed a sharp kick into where he thought the person's ribs might have been.

The man on the ground curled tighter into a ball, in a vain effort at self-preservation. It didn't work, as Kenji kicked him again, and then once more before calmly stepping out of the cupboard and leaving the office.

"Send the photos to the boss," he told Kyota when he met her at the bottom of the stairs.

In his luxury residence overlooking Lake Biwa, on the outskirts of Kyoto, Katashi Goto's phone pinged. It was loud enough on the low side-table next to his futon bed that it awoke him from his slumber. He didn't sleep all that much these days, and three or four hours was enough to suffice. He reached over to grasp his phone from the table with a slender, liver-spotted hand, and with considerable effort, he sat up. He checked the text message that had just arrived and exhaled through his nose; it was the sound an excited pig might make while foraging for truffles.

Slowly, almost as if in instalments, Katashi rose from the futon on weak legs. He shrugged on the thick robe that hung on the back of the master-suite door.

With short, shuffling steps he made his way to his beautifully adorned office. As he stepped through the door, a light automatically came on. He sat his near-emaciated frame behind his desk, easing back into the leather chair. His eyes found the digital clock on the desk.

5:48 am. He pressed the intercom button built into the desk.

"Yes, master?" his servant asked immediately.

"Saki. Bring the bottle."

Chapter Fourteen

"Nooo," Kane yelled. "No... No, I'm... I'm sorry," he muttered as Ridley's hand slipped from his desperate grasp and she tumbled out of sight over the ledge. He scrambled further over the precipice, unwilling to believe his eyes, but he saw her, black hair swirling and legs cartwheeling wildly as she slammed into the gnarly, lethal cliff face.

Kane sat upright, his breath held as his heart thundered in the darkness. A sheen of sweat glimmered on his forehead, despite the cool air in the room. He suddenly inhaled after realising he hadn't drawn in a breath since awakening.

A moment later, he mumbled, "Where are you?"

Kane blinked a few times to clear his eyes and let them become accustomed to the dark. Slowly, he inhaled and exhaled again as the realisation of yet another nightmare settled into his addled mind.

Kane lay back down and reached for the bottle he knew was beside his bed. When his hand failed to find what it sought, he exhaled once more, instantly relieved. He hadn't touched a drop of booze in weeks now, and as the relief flooded through him, he let his eyes close again as he willed his heart rate and breaths to cease racing.

"Alex…" he whispered into the darkness. "I'm sorry…"

It was then he remembered the wild car chase from the previous evening. By some miracle, he and Jae-won had escaped injury and other than being pretty shaken up, and of more concern, still with no idea who had chased them halfway across the province, they had made it back to the temple complex with no further incident. Kane assumed whoever those men were, they had avoided capture. It meant they would still be out there, and might even come here to the—

The flimsy door to his small room suddenly rattled, startling Kane. He checked his watch. 5:45 am.

What the hell?

Kane climbed wearily from the cot and slipped on his robe as the door rattled again. With a knot of concern forming unbidden in his gut, he moved with urgency to swing open the door and was surprised to see a young girl standing there. It took a moment to recognise her in the predawn gloom.

"Ji-yeon? What's going on?"

His mentor's eleven-year-old daughter Ji-yeon said, "Come quickly, Hiram."

"Come now? What is it? What on earth is going on?" The knot of trepidation in Kane's gut now tightened into a rigid ball of fear. "It's the middle of the night, Ji-yeon." Something he saw in her eyes told Kane that didn't matter.

"Please, come." Ji-yeon pulled Kane from the room. He followed the young girl as her little legs made haste towards her father's compound within the main temple complex. When Kane stepped inside, and he saw Jae-won's grave expression, that knot yanked even tighter.

"It's gone," Jae-won said simply.

"What's gone?" Kane asked. "What is it, Jae-won? What the hell's going on?"

After a long silence, Jae-won took a deep breath and fixed his gaze on Kane. "Our soul. The soul of an entire nation. They have taken it."

"Who's taken it? And what even is it? What are you talking about?"

Jae-won slumped down into a chair. He was one of the strongest, most stoic men Kane had ever known, but right now he looked haunted, beaten up, as if some great tragedy had happened. Kane took a seat next to his friend.

"Okay, mate… let's all just take a breath. Now tell me, what on earth is going on?" Kane forced calmness into his words, though he didn't feel at all calm himself.

Jae-won took a couple of deep breaths and looked at Kane. "The… the soul of our people, Hiram. The Tripitaka. It is so important to us, not only culturally, but spiritually. It is our soul. Our identity."

"But isn't that… like, eighty-thousand… what are they, carved wooden blocks, right? Whoever *they* are, they can't have taken them all?"

"No, not all of them. You are right. It is eighty-thousand, and they are carved blocks of wood. My friend in the police, who called to inform me, told me that upon first inspection at least a dozen blocks from each section are missing. Maybe more. They have not yet managed to locate the curator. Hiram, unless the Tripitaka is complete, it is destroyed. You cut out my heart, yes it is only small, but I will die. It is the same principle. At least the temple building housing the collection is not badly damaged."

"Is anyone hurt? There must be guards. Are they okay?"

Kane's forehead scrunched, tension suddenly building behind his eyes.

Jae-won hung his head. Barely above a whisper, he said, "They executed both guards and destroyed the locks. It is a significant undertaking. It… it must be a professional operation."

Kane shook his head. "Who the hell would do something like this? Who *could* do something like this? It doesn't make any sense!"

Jae-won stood up now, a little recovered from what was obviously shock. His voice rose too. "My guess is the Japanese. Or maybe the Chinese. They have both long been jealous of our cultural icon. No Korean citizen would ever steal the Tripitaka. Never. I would never believe that."

Just then, with a thud and a splintering of wood and a smashing of glass, the front door of the humble house crashed inwards, and two masked men clad all in black hustled into the room, guns raised in front of them.

Jae-won's back had been to the door and he was bundled out of the way before he could react. Kane had instinctively grabbed Ju-hye and shielded Jae-won's wife from the intruders. But no one was quick enough to have reached little Ji-yeon. One of the gunmen thrust out a strong arm and yanked the screaming child towards him, and in a flash she was pinned against his legs with a gun held against her pale temple. Tears streamed down her cheeks as an unforgiving hand was clasped over her mouth.

The other guard took a mobile phone from his pocket and pressed a button, then addressed them in harsh, broken English. Although his eyes were largely hidden, he fixed his gaze toward Kane.

"Nobody move or girl dies. Phone call for Mister Kane… it is old friend. He want to ask question…" he said, motioning with his gun towards Kane, a callous glint in his eyes through the slit in the mask. "How is hand?"

Kane's eyes went wide as he automatically glanced at his left hand. The second finger on his left hand was missing above the knuckle, the remaining stump now smooth. It had been shot off in an incident in Japan several years before, by a Yakuza gangster on the island of Miyajima. His throat suddenly went dry and the knot in his stomach turned into a cannon ball as bile crept up his throat.

"No... oh no, no! It can't be..."

"What, Hiram? Who is it?" Unbridled anger edged Jae-won's voice.

Kane shook his head, eyes wide in disbelief. "It's... it's Goto. Katashi Goto. He has been dead for five years."

Chapter Fifteen

Kane felt dizzy. He opened his mouth to speak but no words emerged. His throat felt like a sandpit. Breath was hard to come by.

At gunpoint, the second guard had ushered Jae-won and Ju-hye onto the couch, and as Kane's gaze met his friend's eyes he saw a myriad of emotions there; rage, sadness, confusion... disappointment in Kane.

Not much made Kane waver. He thought it impossible to ever be shocked by life again. He'd been through so much himself... witnessed so much trauma and devastation, he believed he was immune to being shocked. Yet that's how he felt as he took the proffered mobile phone from the armed intruder with an unsteady hand.

He raised it to his ear and listened, still unable to process who he thought it was. Perhaps it was all just a joke? Perhaps it wasn't Katashi, and instead it was one of the mafia don's old gang contacts? That's what Kane hoped. Deep down he knew it wasn't true. He listened to the slow, wheezing breaths of the person on the other end of the line, and though he hadn't yet heard a voice, he knew in his heart who's laboured breaths they were.

It was Katashi Goto.

Kane inhaled then let it go through pursed lips. Finally, he managed to form words. "You're dead!" he stated.

"Hiram Kane. It has been a long time."

"You died. You went to prison, and there, you died."

"Yes, it is true, Hiram. I died at the prison. It was two years ago. Old age, the reports said. It was in the news."

"I know. I saw it. I did not cry."

Katashi Goto made a noise that might have been an attempt at a chuckle. It sounded like a rusted door hinge.

Cancer? Kane thought it might be.

Katashi recovered. "It was such a shame. There were a lot of people at my funeral. It was a sad day for so many. I watched it on the news. I too did not cry. Yet, it is amazing how much influence I still wielded in certain... circles. Power I still wield now."

Kane didn't answer for a long moment as the shock of speaking to a ghost pin-balled in his mind. Finally he managed, "Why are... why are you calling me, Goto? What the hell have you done?"

"The question is not what I have done, although by now I suppose that must be obvious. No, the real question here is... what are you going to do?"

"What do you mean? What has any of this got to do with me? I didn't hurt you, Katashi. From what I remember, it was your own men who betrayed you."

"That is also true. But we yakuza do not—"

"I thought you were a monk?" Kane cut him off. "I thought you'd left that world behind?"

"Ah, you remembered, Hiram. I am truly honoured—"

"Cut the bullshit, Katashi. What the hell have you done?"

"It is true. I did leave that world. For a while. You would have been correct back then," Katashi went on. "I did indeed join the monastery after my... how do you say it in English? Post mortem? But we have a saying here in Japan: *mikka bouzu*. I suppose the closest translation is, 'a monk for three days.' Well, I was a monk for longer than that. But you get the point."

"No, I don't get the point of any of this." Kane was over the shock. Now he was just pissed off. "Why did you call me, Goto? Tell me!"

There followed a brief pause. Kane heard a couple more wheezy breaths before Katashi answered. "You owe me."

Kane almost laughed. "What?! What could I possibly owe you? I didn't hurt anyone in Miyajima. I had to defend myself against your psycho thugs. They tried to kill me. I got the better of them. Hell, you tried to kill me too."

"You don't owe me?" Now it was Katashi's turn to chuckle, though it was a dry and mirthless sound. Then he said, slowly and calmly, "You owe me everything, Hiram Kane. And if you do not give me what I want, I will take everything from you!"

Chapter Sixteen

Kane's mouth gaped like a beached fish.

It was as if all the air had been sucked from his lungs. His chest felt like a vacuum, a void, a bottomless crevasse as his world fell apart around him.

He nearly stumbled on suddenly weak knees, but righted himself at the last moment. Yet his arms slumped to his sides and the mobile phone slipped from his grasp and bounced a couple of times then skidded across the cold stone floor.

Why me? was his immediate thought. *Why does this shit always happen to me?*

Self-doubts rose as they so often did in Kane's mind. That old familiar, nagging doubt that it was some kind of penance for some previous selfish behaviour. Some form of enigmatic punishment for prior sins. Yet Kane believed himself a good man, and, he hoped, a noble soul, with integrity and steadfast honesty. His friends would tell you they'd never met a more genuine person, never known anyone so thoughtful, so inherently good. That's what he believed, yet doubts began to shroud him like an icy mist.

Kane wasn't a religious man. Yet once again, it seemed as if some invisible forces beyond the normal realm had conspired to act against him, at a time when he was doing his best to lay low and to become more or less anonymous in the world, both his world and the worlds of others.

Jae-won looked Kane pointedly in the eye. *What the fuck is going on?* he asked with pleading eyes.

Kane held the gaze for several seconds, inhaling deeply of the air his lungs lacked, and then letting it out slowly from between pursed lips. After another deep breath and slow exhalation, Kane nodded at his friend.

Raising the mobile to his face again, he said slowly, "What is it you want, Katashi Goto? What could I possibly do to help you? More importantly, why? You tried to kill me, as I mentioned." Kane glanced at the negative space his missing finger once occupied. "And you killed two of my friends. Good people, Goto. Innocent people. And now you dare to break into this home and threaten more innocent people, including a mother and a young child? No, Goto. I won't do it. I will not help you."

Surely the bastard would've expected this response. Yet, knowing the former Yakuza don's history, Kane suspected it wouldn't matter.

"Yes, you *will* help me, Hiram Kane." Katashi took a raspy breath, that whistled like air through a reed stalk. "It is a simple task that I will ask, especially of a man of your... special talents."

Kane heard Katashi Goto struggle for breath. *It really might be cancer,* he mused, but remained silent.

Katashi continued. "You will steal the Vase of Heaven. It will not be difficult for you. When you have it, you will trade it. A simple transaction, one object for another. In fact, it is a better deal than that. One object for many thousands of objects. In return for the artefact, I will give Korea back its precious Tripitaka."

"It's... that is insane, Goto. It must be the most heavily guarded object in all Korea." He glanced at Jae-won.

Jae-won narrowed his eyes. "What does he want?" he whispered.

Without warning, the second thug backhanded Jae-won, stunning him into silence.

"Do not speak!" the gunman demanded.

"Forget it!" Kane barked into the phone. "It can't be done."

"What does he want?" Jae-won said more urgently, this time leaving no room for Kane to avoid the question. Again, the guard hit him, this time with a brutal forehand slap and Jae-won rocked back against the sofa, unhurt but seething through gritted teeth. Ju-hye stifled a scream beside him as Jae-won placed a strong hand on her knee.

Abstractedly, Kane noted that given just half a chance, even a mere quarter, his friend could rip that bastard's head off.

Kane fixed his gaze on Jae-won. "He wants... he wants the Japanese artefact known as the Vase of Heaven." Kane spoke quietly, as if Katashi were in the room.

Jae-won stared at the thug but remained silent for many seconds. His eyes darted about, though he wasn't looking at anything present. To Kane it was as if his friend's mind were analysing something, internally, and yet far away all at once. This time he held his tongue, kept his rage intact. Kane saw how terrified Jae-won's wife and child were, and knew his friend could not risk the guards doing something unimaginable to them. Kane understood the need for them both to stay passive.

Jae-won fixed onto Kane's eyes with his own and nodded decisively, as if to say: *Yes, we can get that item!*

Kane was unsure, but removed his hand from the phone and raised it once more to his face.

"I need some time to think about—"

"No, Hiram. You do not get time to think. Only to act. I am afraid time is something I am running out of…" Katashi emitted a small hacking cough. "Which means it is not something I am prepared to share. You have seventy-two hours. Seventy-two hours to get that for which I have asked. Or the heart and soul of Korea will become a pile of ash."

Chapter Seventeen

Heung-min heard them coming, and in advance had curled himself into a tight ball before one of the kidnappers had come into the room and kicked him a few times in the chest area. He had grunted in pain and yelled out. Yet, in truth, the kicks had done little damage and had barely impacted his body. Heung-min was built like his father, Jae-won. He was tall and broad-shouldered, with a powerful chest, and biceps that had been forged over hundreds of hours in the university gym. He was proud of his physique, which felt as if it had been carved from granite.

Heung-min had always been a natural athlete, and played for the university's soccer team. Like his father, he too was an expert in the Korean martial art of tae-kwon-do, though not yet a master, like his dad. For now he was focusing on his studies and tae-kwon-do had been placed on the back burner, though he still trained twice a week, mostly for the discipline aspects it brought. One day he would attain his master's belt. It was a family tradition he was keen to uphold. Secretly, he even hoped to surpass his father's skill, though ego was frowned upon in their family, so he kept that ambition to himself. For now.

What this all meant was that despite the assailant thinking his captive was suffering—he had certainly given out the impression he'd been hurt—Heung-min was actually doing pretty well under the circumstances. He was more or less unharmed, despite making it appear otherwise. Perhaps more importantly, mentally he was as yet untroubled. He found that he wasn't afraid, and other than the initial shock of being kidnapped on the street on his way to university that morning, he remained stoic. That was one of the facets of his tae-kwon-do training; the ability to remain calm under pressure, to retain your discipline and to think clearly when human nature screamed at you to run and hide. To flight rather than fight.

Not Heung-min. Not today!

What Heung-min knew was that no matter who these people were—he thought they were Japanese, but they'd hardly spoken in his presence, which was probably a deliberate ploy on their part—if he got a chance to fight any of them, one-on-one, then he knew he could win. From what little he'd been able to discern during the frenetic kidnapping, he believed none of the individuals were bigger or stronger than he was, and disregarding the chance, or likelihood, they were armed, he could overcome any single one of them. He just needed an opportunity.

But who were they? Heung-min was of no significance to anyone. He felt certain it was just a random kidnapping. He almost laughed. His family had no real capital wealth. His father's university pension was modest at best. His mum had almost exclusively been a housewife, like many Korean mothers. Now they ran a temple, where guests could stay for free. Unlike many of the world's other major religions,

Buddhism was definitely a not-for-profit organisation. He felt a smile creep to his lips, but his predicament wasn't funny. Not funny at all.

So why him? He thought about what might have been different lately. What had changed in the lives of himself and of his family? Nothing. Nothing obvious he could think of. Of course, his father's friend Hiram had come for a visit and had been staying with them for a few weeks…

Hiram Kane. Kane was the only uncommon denominator in their lives during recent weeks. What could Hiram possibly have to do with anything? Heung-min knew Kane was somewhat of a celebrity in certain circles. He also knew that his reasons for visiting and staying with the family weren't altogether good reasons. But he knew Hiram, had known him most of his life. He considered him a kind of uncle to himself and his sister Ji-yeon. The man was practically family. He knew Hiram felt the same about them.

Still, now that nagging seed of doubt had been planted, Heung-min couldn't deny the likely fact that Hiram Kane being in Korea was somehow relevant to the situation. Not in a nefarious way. Never. Heung-min knew Hiram Kane was a good man and one of his father's closest and oldest friends. Yet, his father often joked how Kane was always getting himself into trouble.

What trouble is he in now?

Heung-min put thoughts of Kane to one side as he heard the lock engage to the storage room they were keeping him in, and the door creak open. He held himself still, consciously tensing his significant muscles in case a less-than-stray boot came his way.

The footsteps padded towards him slowly, and then paused. Whoever they belonged to had stopped, and

Heung-min braced for impact. When none came, after a few seconds he took his chance.

"I am hungry. I need water," he said in flawless English, certain the kidnappers weren't native Koreans. He listened, and was surprised when he heard what sounded like a tray being placed on the floor beside him.

"Then eat," came a woman's voice. It was cold, and devoid of any emotion. "How you can eat that kimchi shit is beyond me."

Heung-min listened as the footsteps moved away and the door closed behind the woman, but not before she had switched on the light. He leaned away from the radiator and shifted his body, moving his head towards the tray. He immediately took several long and nourishing slurps of the water through the straw in the open bottle, then grabbed up a bite of kimchi. The hot chili sauce that doused the potent fermented cabbage dribbled down his chin. He didn't care. He was starving.

Heung-min spent the next few minutes eating the rest of the kimchi and the kimbap—seaweed-wrapped sushi rolls—and downing the rest of the water. When he was finished, feeling energised and now certain he was safe for at least another twenty-four hours, he leaned back against the radiator and began to plot how he could get the hell out of there.

Chapter Eighteen

Kane stared at Jae-won, his emotions raging.

How was this happening? Again?!

On the other end of the phone was a madman he had believed dead for several years. Yet there he was, and Kane had no doubt it was really Katashi Goto—he'd recognise that wheezing, raspy, callous voice anywhere—demanding something Kane believed was impossible. Something he *knew* was impossible.

On the other hand, sitting close to him now and with a look of grim determination etched into his weathered face, was a good friend, a man he trusted implicitly, and who was steadfastly telling him that the impossible was, in fact, possible.

Kane's mind raced with the weight of the situation and he faltered, before common sense gave way to fear, and at the same time, gave way to the thin shred of hope he felt.

Kane turned away from Jae-won and addressed the former Yakuza don. "It cannot be done, Katashi," he said into the phone. "It is impossible." Kane stated it as a simple fact. That is what he believed. "And you will not get away with this. I will not help you."

Katashi Goto sighed. Unerringly patiently to Kane's ears, Katashi said, "Yes, Mr Kane, you will help me. You will do as I say."

Jae-won inhaled and said quietly, in Japanese, "Please, may I speak?"

The thug with his gun pointing at Jae-won and Ju-hye looked to the other. That man nodded, and the second thug grunted. "Speak."

Jae-won nodded back respectfully. "I know that object. The Vase of Heaven. It was allegedly... it was stolen by Korean thieves a few decades ago," he corrected, playing the guilt card. "It has remained a source of tension between our two countries ever since."

"But if it's locked away in the museum, we can't get it. Right?" Kane's mind momentarily drifted to a time back in the Czech Republic, when another crazed criminal had set him the impossible task of stealing a priceless painting from a museum in Prague. He had somehow lived to tell the tale. "What the hell am I even thinking? Of course it can't be done!"

"Tell them we can get it," Jae-won told Kane emphatically. Then in Japanese, he pleaded with the thugs. "Tell your boss we can get it!"

"Are you serious?" Kane almost growled. It was a sound born of sheer frustration, one made when the blindingly obvious simply could not be seen by others around you, when you felt so alone in the world and the only one left with any sense of logic was you.

"You are insane, Katashi. It can *not* be done." Kane spun and glared at his friend, too. He aimed his next words at both Jae-won and the Yakuza man. "Are you both mad? It simply cannot be done, and this conversation is over."

"No!" Jae-won seethed. "Do not end the call. Trust me on this one, son, trust me. It can be done. I… something about this is… well, we have no choice, I can feel it. Tell him. Tell that bast… tell him we will get him what he wants. Tell him now, Hiram!"

Jae-won had spoken with such sincerity and intensity, that it left Kane in no doubt that even if he refused to be any part of this madness, Jae-won would take it upon himself. Kane couldn't allow that. He knew Katashi Goto. He knew what the man was capable of. He would not allow Jae-won to venture into this sick game alone. He exhaled and nodded slowly, letting his shoulders relax. Kane raised the phone to his ear.

"Your friend is wise, Mr Kane." Katashi's voice was so quiet Kane had to strain to hear. Quiet, like a snake. Dripping with poison and malice. "And you would be wise to listen. After all, do you want to be the man responsible for one of the world's most important cultural treasures being destroyed and lost for all time?"

Chapter Nineteen

Kane felt the enormous weight of Katashi Goto's words pressing down on his shoulders. They swirled in his gut. Dried his throat. Rang in his ears like tubular bells on steroids.

The worst thing was, he knew the man was right. There was no way he could just step back and not act. He couldn't. He simply was not built that way. Worse still was that Katashi also knew this. It's why he had risen from the dead all this time later, to use Kane, to utilise the skills he knew Kane possessed.

When they had first met on Kane's ill-fated visit to Miyajima, Japan, it had been Kane's misfortune to get caught up in the then Yakuza don's nefarious scheme. Kane had been on a visit to the pretty island off the Japanese coast, doing touristy things, a rare chance to enjoy time off from his busy schedule at the tourism conference at which he'd been speaking in the nearby city of Hiroshima.

He had been an innocent bystander one minute, then had somehow found himself risking his life to prevent a scheme to steal a priceless suit of samurai armour at the Itsukushima Shrine Museum. Innocent people had died in that wild theft gone mad, along with some of Katashi's men, one of whom he'd witnessed literally getting beheaded. Ultimately, the priceless artefact had been saved, though the loss of life had haunted Kane since. He had been an innocent pawn then, as he was now. And yet, here he was, once more at the mercy of a deranged old man.

Once again an overwhelming desire to turn his back on it all and disappear rose to the surface. He was embittered by it, sick of being told what to do by people who shouldn't hold any power over him. Why couldn't people just leave him alone? It's why he'd disappeared for a few months to Cambodia earlier in the year. He thought that out there, far away on little-known Rabbit Island off the coast, he'd be free of it all. Anonymous. Unreachable. How wrong he had been. Then he'd tried to disappear again, coming to Korea and not telling anyone where he was, other than those people in this room with him now.

Wrong again, Kane, he mused. *Why am I always wrong?*

Sighing inwardly, Kane once more raised the phone to his ear. He listened, again hearing Katashi's low, rasping breaths. Kane didn't wish anyone dead. He wasn't that kind of person. And yet, for the first time in his life he wished Katashi hadn't survived the fall from the helicopter in Miyajima that day. Hadn't survived his stint in a Japanese high-security prison. Had actually died for real when he'd somehow faked his death. Kane shook his head.

"Okay, I'll do it," was his simple message to Katashi Goto. Kane's shoulders sagged again, unable to prevent it, sick with the knowledge that he was once more bowing to the whim of an unhinged, dangerous madman.

What he heard next chilled him to his core.

"Yes, Mr Kane, you will do it. As I knew you would. And let me add just one more piece of inspiration for you, in case you should unwisely change your mind. Or, you know, get cold feet…"

Kane closed his eyes. He didn't need any extra motivation. His hands, morally if not physically, were already tied. "Get on with it, Katashi."

"You will secure that item of which I ask. Because if you do not, your friend's son will die."

Chapter Twenty

Kane blinked. Then again.

Katashi's voice had faded away, replaced now by the sound of waves crashing against a rocky beach, whooshing and roaring in his ears as all other noise disappeared. He staggered a little, as he had before, but this time he dropped to one knee, somehow managing not to collapse completely. He gagged as acidic bile rose, burning the inside of his throat. He sucked in a wild breath, desperate to force the bile down.

No, no… no…

From his half-kneeling position his eyes flew first to Jae-won, and he saw a man who knew something abhorrent had happened.

Kane let his eyes drift to Ji-yeon. Jae-won's wife sat there, rigid, staring at him, one hand clamped to her mouth and the other clutched protectively against her chest. All he could see were her brown eyes, now wide with what could only be described as a look of horror residing there.

His eyes darted back at Jae-won, tears forming in

Kane's own eyes and Jae-won's face twisted in fear as he registered the shock and trauma now etched onto Kane's features.

Kane slumped from his knees onto one side, unable to prevent the phone from skittering across the stone floor. He lay there, arms together, fists intertwined as if locking them in case they went on a violent rampage. It had been known before, when Kane found himself in his darkest moments. Jae-won recognised the systems of pure shock immediately.

"Hiram? What is it, Hiram?" Jae-won's words were urgent, yet uttered calmly. "What did they say? What did that man say to you, Hiram?"

"I'm... I am so sorry. They..." Kane's voice trailed off. He was unable to say what he needed to say. How had this happened? These people didn't deserve this. No one deserved to learn something like this had happened to one of their children. And yet, it was somehow his fault. Somehow, though Kane didn't yet exactly know how, or what, he was responsible for whatever dire situation Heung-min was now in.

"Hiram, come on, pull yourself together!" Jae-won spoke louder now, barely concealing anger that threatened to spill forth. It wasn't aimed at Kane, but he had no other outlet for it. "What's going on, son?" Jae-won said a little more gently, trying to coax some sense out of his one-time student and long-time friend. He glanced over his shoulder at his wife, who had edged a little closer. Her eyes retained their haunted look and Jae-won's heart broke at her fear. Yet somehow she found it within herself to address Kane, the gunmen looking on callously at the interplay between stricken, traumatised friends.

"Hiram? It is so okay," she soothed. "We know you did

nothing bad. But... you must tell us. What happened? You must tell us, Hiram. What is going on?"

"They have... it's... They've taken him."

"What? Who has taken who?" Jae-won's face betrayed his fears.

"Katashi has... They've taken him. They have taken Heung-min."

Ji-yeon's hands again flew to her mouth and an unnerving high-pitched groan escaped through her fingers.

"They have your son."

Kane heard the dial tone droning from the mobile phone and lowered the handset, his eyes finding Jae-won's. "He is gone," he said, his voice a monotone.

"Seventy-two hours," the guard clutching little Ji-yeon against him stated for all in the small room to hear. "Do not fail!" With that, he shoved the frightened girl into her father's arms, and a moment later they ducked out of the destroyed doorway, and were gone.

Just seconds later, Jae-won darted out after them, but like wraiths of the night, they were nowhere to be seen. Kane had recovered and risen and he too charged out of the door, ready to attack the bastards who had dared enter his friend's property and threaten his family. Yet, like Jae-won, he was bewildered by their apparent disappearing act.

"Mua?" Jae-won mumbled, reverting to his native Korean and turning to Kane. *What?*

Jae-won staggered. Like Kane had before, Jae-won felt his legs buckle a little and it was only his natural athleticism and his mastery of balance that kept him upright.

"What?" he muttered again. "Taken?"

Ji-yeon began crying, huge, wracking sobs that stripped the air from her lungs, each sob ending in a kind of wailing noise that broke Kane's heart as he went back inside their humble home house. He had recovered from his initial moment of dread-shock and now he knew he had to stand up and be counted, for his friends, for their little girl, and for their son, Heung-min.

His next thought was that Heung-min was a tough kid, a physical specimen who could look after himself. Instantly, though, Kane knew none of that mattered. Katashi Goto, and anyone he had working for him, weren't programmed like normal people. They had a different moral code to regular, good people. People like Heung-min. His family. Alex Ridley.

People like me?

Kane searched the floor for the mobile phone. Maybe he could try and redial the number. He had to try something. He spotted the phone—it now rested on a side table—and returned to the main living area to find Jae-won crouched next to Ju-hye, who was sitting on the sofa with her legs tucked to her chest, her arms wrapped tightly around her daughter, trying her best to control her own sobs and comfort the little girl, who clearly didn't quite understand what was happening but knew it wasn't good.

Jae-won stared hard at Kane. Kane saw he was fighting a range of emotions. His eyes flickered from Kane to his wife and daughter, then off into some unknown scene beyond the confines of the house, then settled back on Kane. Kane noticed he was controlling his breathing using the method he had taught Kane during their years of taekwon-do training; one the master, the other, the apprentice.

Looking hard at Kane, Jae-won spoke. "Call him. Do it now."

Kane nodded. He was about to try and work out the redial feature when the phone rang, its shrill tone breaking the near-silence and startling them all. Kane answered on the second ring.

"Katashi? Katashi, are you there?" Kane couldn't hear the tell-tale laboured breathing from before. "Katashi, how do I know you're not bluffing? Can you prove you have Heung-min? Katash—"

There was a click, followed by a short pause, and then a second click, as if a different line had been connected.

"Op-pa?" came a man's voice. *Dad?* The word was steady but taut with emotion. Kane didn't think he sounded afraid. He handed the phone to Jae-won, who snatched it from him.

"Heung-min?" cried Jae-won. In Korean, he said, "Is that you? Are you okay, son? Heung-min?"

"Yes father, it is me. They grabbed me and threw me in a van outside university. I'm okay. I am not hurt. I'm sorry I was not stronger. I'm—"

"Heung-Min?" yelled Jae-won, but the line clicked, then fell silent, and Katashi's calm voice came back on the line.

"You see, Hiram," Katashi said as if he were speaking to Kane, "this is not a bluff. So now you understand why you must do as I have asked. Seventy-two hours. Not a moment longer, or it is very simple... the boy dies." The line went dead.

Jae-won breathed deep. His heart pounded against his ribs and adrenaline coursed through his veins as an icy electricity tingled in his fingers. He stared at Kane, eyes brimming with tears of rage and heartbreak in equal measures.

"I'm going to kill him."

Chapter Twenty-One

Kane nodded. He wasn't exactly a violent man, not these days. He'd been involved in so many scrapes with violent men over the recent years, however—and one very violent, psychotic woman—that it had become par for the course on his work travels and adventures, though every time he sought to find another, more peaceful way out. A less violent denouement. A better way.

However, Kane knew that deep down, if he was really honest with himself, that's not how he was built. He despised injustice. He hated bullies. He had always sided with the underdog, of which he had considered himself the same so many times. He was a natural fighter, and in another life, in antiquity, he might have fancied himself a warrior. It's why he'd taken up tae-kwon-do in the first place, though not for the fighting skills. Rather, it appealed more for the discipline it required, for the ability to control his anger and rage, and not use them. Jae-won had been the perfect teacher.

Still, it was those survival instincts, that innate need for justice, that were the overriding emotions coursing through him now as he listened to Jae-won state he was going to kill Katashi Goto. Kane couldn't help but agree with his friend.

The two men shared that moment, glares meeting glares with such intensity that anyone observing the scene without any context of the situation might have believed they were about to attack each other. In truth, it was simply two men fighting their own emotions, their own demons, battling against an innate need for justice, or revenge, and instead trying to contain all of that in order to come up with a better, more logical plan moving forward.

After long, tense moments fraught with dangerous energy, Jae-won finally exhaled and closed his eyes for a moment. He then opened them again and stepped forward, gently taking Kane's forearms in his hands.

"We know you are not to blame for any of this, Hiram, though I see in your eyes you believe it to be different. Come, let us walk outside a while."

Kane nodded. His hammering pulse had reduced to a gentle drumming and his breaths had slowed to their normal rate. He waited while Jae-won went and spoke quietly to his wife for a moment. Kane couldn't help notice Ju-hye eyeballing him over her husband's shoulder with such scrutiny that he couldn't handle it and stepped outside to wait.

He glanced around the temple courtyard, still deserted at this early hour. He then scanned the slowly lightening sky and was alarmed to see it looked as if snow clouds were forming to the east, drifting in from what the Japanese called the Sea of Japan but what the Koreans knew was really the East Sea. *Their* East Sea.

Kane heard the door of Jae-won's home click shut and

turned to see his friend approaching carrying two thick coats.

"Snow is coming. Maybe an hour. Put this on."

Kane gratefully took the proffered coat but didn't fail to notice the cool, efficient way Jae-won had spoken. Gone was the convivial, soft-natured tone his friend usually used. In its place was a hard-edged, clipped pronunciation. Like the razor-sharp edge of a Silla-dynasty sword.

"Who is this man?" Jae-won said, getting straight to the point. "Who is he, really? Why is he doing this to our family? And to you?" Jae-won glanced sideways at Kane as they walked.

Kane didn't know what to say. In truth, he didn't know the answer. He and Katashi had crossed paths a few years ago. Kane had been instrumental in foiling the one-time Yakuza overlord's attempts at stealing a priceless artefact he claimed belonged to his ancestor, thus, his own property. It was later proved it wasn't his at all, and had just been a nefarious ruse to get his hands on the valuable object. None of that mattered now. Now it was different. Last time, Kane had simply been in a very wrong place at a very wrong time. This time it was premeditated. This time, the stakes were even higher. Now Katashi was using Kane, rather than battling against him.

Kane had always thought that Katashi would have made greater enemies than himself over the man's half century of admittedly horrendous criminal activities. Surely there had been rival gang leaders, he thought, or even entire organisations that had actively tried to destroy Katashi, and probably even kill him. Kane had merely done the right thing at the time, something he hoped anyone would have tried to do given the chance. He certainly didn't believe he was worthy of some kind of years-long vendetta.

And yet, here he was.

"My friend, I'm not sure why he's doing this to your family," Kane said to Jae-won. "I only know that he is using me somehow, and unfortunately your family is caught up in it. It is nothing personal... it's just—"

"Not personal? How can it not be personal? He has taken Heung-min! He has our son!"

"Sorry, I meant yes, *now* it is personal, but he didn't choose you and Heung-min because of you. It was because of me. I'm... I am so sorry."

Kane's head dropped low, but Jae-won snapped him out of it when he said:

"There is not time for self-pity here, Hiram. You know that. So I ask again. Who is he?"

Kane nodded and proceeded to fill Jae-won in on Katashi Goto, briefly outlining who he was and what had happened in Miyajima those years ago, as well as some of the dark backstory of his callous life of crime. Jae-won had of course heard most of it before, but now that it was pertinent to him he wanted to hear it again. He needed to.

He had to learn about his enemy.

After some back and forth regarding the back-from-the-dead former Yakuza boss, Kane asked the obvious elephant-in-the-room question.

"How can we possibly achieve what Katashi asked? Surely it is not possible."

Kane felt Jae-won's gaze before he turned to face his friend. "We can do it, Hiram." Jae-won's words remained direct and cold, to the point.

Glancing again at his friend as they walked, and noticing his stoic expression, Kane knew Jae-won truly believed it. Despite his grave doubts, Kane nodded.

"What choice do we have anyway?" Jae-won added. "None."

Kane stopped walking and turned to Jae-won, just as the first flakes of snow fell from the gloomy sky.

It was a simple question he'd asked, and an even simpler answer, of which Kane was in complete agreement. They had no choice. Jae-won's son was being held hostage. They would do whatever it took to get him back safe.

To get him back alive.

Chapter Twenty-Two

Katashi Goto climbed carefully out of the rear seat of his chauffeur-driven limo and, once he'd gathered his balance, leaning on the vehicle, he paused.

It was colder than he'd expected, and though the forecast on the TV suggested there would be snow around Kyoto, he hadn't believed them. It was a trust thing. He had rarely trusted anyone who claimed to know more than he did, especially those clowns at the weather centres. His natural propensity to mistrust anything and anyone had served him well, and had seen him rise from lowly foot-soldier as a young lad, all the way up to undisputed boss of the largest Yakuza gang outside of Tokyo.

His power then had known no barrier, especially not a human one, and it had provided him with a fruitful and, he could even say, a rewarding life. That was until a certain Englishman had gotten in the fucking way, and Katashi had ended up first in the hospital, then seeing out the rest of his years behind bars in prison.

Until he'd died.

He still thought of that event as one of his masterstrokes in a long series of what he considered nothing short of genius choices that had seen him scale the heights—and depths—of the Japanese underworld. Humility was *not* one of his strengths, and he knew that lack of humility also served him well.

There was nothing in this life for those who waited for things to happen to them. He firmly believed to this day. No, Katashi was a man who went out and took what he wanted. His endeavours in Korea now were cut from the same cloth. He had decided he wanted the Tripitaka Koreana. He still wasn't entirely sure why, other than the fact that the Japanese had been trying and failing to claim it for themselves for centuries. Being the first to succeed sounded fun. Though, in truth, Katashi didn't need a reason. Men like Katashi Goto rarely had to justify their desires. They simply desired something, and took what they wanted.

Even Katashi had to admit that this desire was a little ambitious. Taking the samurai suit had been easy in comparison. At least until that man had got in the way.

That man.

Hiram Kane.

So he'd decided to use Kane this time, to manipulate the man's weaknesses Katashi had learned about in Miyajima. He'd been very fortunate to have learned Kane was in Korea. Katashi maintained a network of contacts all over eastern Asia, in all the major cities of Japan, China and Korea, even as far south as Hong Kong and beyond that, in Singapore, Bangkok and Kuala Lumpur. One of those contacts in Korea had informed Katashi that Hiram Kane had entered the country several weeks ago. It was a stroke of luck, but then again, Katashi was of the belief that great men made their own luck. And he was a great man. Of that he had no doubt.

So, not only was he able to utilise Kane to execute his plan, but he would finally be able to exact a revenge he had once never thought possible.

In fact, if he were being honest with himself, he cared more about the revenge than he did for the artefact.

He stepped away from the limousine and shuffled slowly across the deserted road to stand upon his private stretch of gravelly shore, upon which the placid waters of Lake Biwa settled. It was just a short drive down the private road from his mansion high on the hill overlooking the lake. He glanced along the shore and saw dark, heavy, purple-tinged clouds billowing over the mountains to the north. Snow!

Maybe... maybe not.

"Katashi-san, we should go back. Snow is coming." It was his driver who had called out from beside the limo. Katashi ignored him.

It was a bit risky coming out in public, although this stretch of road rarely got any traffic. Risky because, after all, he *was* officially dead. And if he wasn't dead, he would be in prison.

In truth he was probably unrecognisable to any normal citizen. Gone were the strong yet lithe muscles he'd retained until well into his seventies. Prison food and, more recently, cancer had seen to that. And gone was his trademark white beard and top knot. At the time of his incarceration, after a stint in the maximum-security hospital recovering from his wounds after being thrown from a helicopter and then battling Kane, he had still been able to look after himself physically. Older age, and a lifetime of hard living, had finally caught up with the former mafia don and he knew, though he hated to admit it, he didn't have many revolutions of the sun left.

A year, the doctor had told him then. Again, that trust thing. Katashi thought it was more like weeks, perhaps a month or two. People lied to Katashi because they feared him. It was difficult being so powerful, not knowing who to trust. So he trusted no one but himself.

Katashi felt a snowflake settle on his cheek, the first of the season. *The fuckers were right,* he mused and almost smiled. He didn't. Katashi Goto rarely smiled.

Kane, on the other hand... he trusted Hiram Kane. Though adversaries, he admired the man. Kane had shown no fear on the island, despite being faced with impossible odds. He had shown courage and integrity, when Katashi's own men were the ones to betray him. So yes, he admired the Englishman who had almost ruined him.

Almost...

Yet, while Katashi still drew breath, and while blood still pumped through his veins, however weakly these days, he desired two more things in his life; two more things to achieve before happily passing over to join his ancestors in the afterlife.

Getting his hands on the Vase of Heaven, and delivering a crushing blow to the Korean nation by defiling their most prized asset, the Tripitaka Koreana. Those two counted as one.

The real prize?

Revenge over Hiram Kane.

Chapter Twenty-Three

"Let's start at the beginning." Kane tuned to Jae-won. "What do you know of the object he wants?"

Jae-won's hand moved to his chin. A thoughtful look settled in his eyes. He inhaled, then let it out slowly, his breath forming as mist in front of his face. "Not a great deal in truth."

They had returned to the family dwelling and Jae-won checked in with his wife, who seemed to have calmed somewhat and was displaying the stoic fortitude Kane had long admired both of her, and of the Koreans he had met over the years in general. He felt enormous relief when she handed him a mug of steaming tea, and while she hadn't exactly smiled, her judgmental glare was gone.

"Come, sit by the fire," she muttered.

Jae-won ushered Kane onto a cushion by the open fire place, that provided the only heat in the room other than the small stove in the kitchen. They weren't a poor family by any means, and in fact Jae-won still owned a couple of moderately successful businesses. But they were living a somewhat austere life by choice, choosing to live at the temple complex and lead by example to their many visiting guests, mostly foreigners eager to experience a more or less monastic life, if only for a short time.

"I know that the vase artefact is revered by the Japanese, though it has been at the Gyeongju National Museum here in Korea since the nineties."

"Is it big? I mean, can it even be removed?" Kane had no idea.

Finally, Jae-won cracked a half grin, though it was fleeting. He raised his hands and held them no more than eight inches apart. His eyebrows rose in question.

"Size is not everything," Kane confirmed, and Jae-won chuckled.

"Yes, it can be removed."

It was a short-lived, lighthearted moment, but it benefitted both men and helped removed any lingering tension between the old friends.

"So we can physically remove it. That is only useful if we can extract it from its secured display area. Right?"

Jae-won nodded.

"Although I haven't knowingly seen that actual piece"—Kane had been to the spectacular museum before, that offered cutting edge facilities in a traditional-style building—"I remain sure it is not possible, not without setting off half the alarms in the city. The police would be there in minutes."

Jae-won nodded once more. "True. I did not say it was not going to be easy. Yes, there will be alarms. I believe there are even security guards. But do not forget where we are, son. This is Korea. A land of honour and integrity. Crime rates are low here. You know that."

"Yes, I know, they're low, but they are not zero. Korea has its share of criminals."

Kane had said that last sentence with more venom than he'd meant. He looked away. His mind drifted to images of his love, Alex Ridley, and the man who had once kidnapped her like a coward, taking her down when there was no one there to help her. His name was Do-hyun Kim. He was Korean.

As if understanding what Kane was thinking—Jae-won knew all about the terrible events in India and Tibet a few years ago—he simply nodded. But there was no time to waste.

"I say we go to the museum and check it out. It will be open at ten this morning. If we leave now we will be the first visitors. Okay? Hiram?"

Kane's attention was brought back into the conversation. He shook his head and put thoughts of Ridley and the sleazy Korean human trafficker aside.

"Yes, let's do it. If we go now we might beat the worst of the weather."

An hour later Jae-won pulled his car to a stop in the car park of Anapji Pond, the famous royal temple complex directly across the highway from the Gyeongju National Museum.

As predicted, snow had begun to fall in heavier swathes and though not that bad yet, it had kept traffic to a minimum on the drive over from Golgulsa in the mountains by the coast. As it turned out they were still early, so they grabbed takeaway coffees from a brave seller huddled in his coffee cart, and hustled back into Jae-won's car.

"So, what's the plan?" Kane asked, the hint of a grin

crinkling his eyes. "Storm the place, all karate-chops blazing?" The tension had risen once more on the drive over and though he knew it was a little risky, it was an attempt to lighten the mood. He waited, nervous of Jae-won's reaction.

Jae-won met his eyes. Deadpan, he said, "I can't believe you'd say something like that at a time like this. I am very disappointed in you."

Kane's head dropped and he averted his eyes. Reaching out a hand, he said, "I'm sorry... I was only trying to—"

"I mean, why use karate when we both know tae-kwon-do is a much more effective way of disabling security guards." Jae-won's face remained neutral, and only the minutest of curves in the corner of his lips betrayed him.

Kane exhaled, then grinned. "Bastard. You really had me there." Kane took a sip of his coffee, but Jae-won's next words grabbed his attention.

"We need to case the museum, but subtly. We can go in today, sure, but we have to act normally. We are just two interested visitors, appreciating the wonderful artefacts. We can work out where any security cameras might be, and then make our best plan of how to proceed. My thought is that we return at night—tonight—after dark and when everyone has left."

Kane nodded, but he had to ask. "And security? Will there be actual security guards on patrol?" Kane didn't know, but he suspected there would be, considering just how important many of the artefacts and cultural treasures on display in the museum were. Despite the comments earlier about how passive and law-abiding Koreans generally were, there surely still had to be high-level security in place.

"Probably. Maybe one or two, perhaps patrolling the perimeter. I do not believe there will be any actual guards inside the building, though. As you know, Koreans are not known for their museum robberies."

"I am inclined to agree with that," Kane said, and nodded.

"We might be a respectful people, with some of the world's lowest crime rates, but there are always bad apples everywhere. Humanity just can't help itself. Still, even though physical security might be limited here, don't forget we are also one of the world's most tech-savvy nations. Digital security is bound to be very tight."

Kane knew that was an understatement, which is why he'd feared all along it couldn't be done. As he sat there now, with the enormity of the task ahead looming large before them, he knew it was insanity to even try. Equally, however, he knew that despite the obvious issues they'd face, they still had zero choice. They simply had to try. The pensive, anxious and fearful expression etched all over his old friend's face left no doubt about that.

"I'm sure Heung-min is fine," Kane said. He hoped it wasn't a lie. "He's a smart kid. A strong young man. He knows how to take care of himself. He had the best mentor!"

Jae-won nodded, his gaze settling on his former protégé. "You are right. For now. He's is a tough boy, it is true. It is his ageing father I am worried about."

Chapter Twenty-Four

Kane and Jae-won paid their nominal entry fees and entered the impressive museum building before they'd even seen any other visitors. The high ceiling of the stunning entry foyer echoed their footsteps back at them as they strolled through on their way to the exhibits. If the circumstances were any different Kane would have been in his element. He was with a good friend, on foreign shores, and surrounded by stunning examples of high Korean culture, ranging from royal crowns and headdresses, to glimmering weapons such as swords, spears and knives. Spectacular porcelain and earthenware vases also offered detailed insights into the skill of ancient Korean craftsmen and women, and Kane, as he always did when visiting such places, marvelled at the ability of humanity to be so technically and artistically high-minded while at the same time remaining cruel and selfish, and basically bastards, to one another; man's inhumanity to his fellow man.

"We're getting close to the item we came to see," Jae-won said quietly as they passed from one upstairs gallery to another. By now a few other visitors had filtered into the museum, among them a gaggle of noisy school kids, evidently happy to be anywhere but actually in school. Kane didn't blame them. Despite continuing his own education as far as a single semester short of attaining his master's degree, Kane had never been comfortable in the education system. He considered himself not a scholar, but a hands-on learner, a trait inherited from his late, great grandfather Hiram Snr, a man he admired and missed greatly since his cold-blooded murder in Egypt several months previous.

"Understood," Kane replied, feeling the first beat of adrenalin give his pulse a boost.

Jae-won led the pair of them over to the right flank of a large display gallery. The room was long and wide, more like a grand hall. The artefact in question sat alone in its own display case. It wasn't until Kane reached within several feet of the case that he actually saw the object nestled on its stand: The Vase of Heaven. Jae-won was right, and he got the joke; it could easily be moved. Kane grinned inwardly. The modest-looking vase was perhaps twelve inches tall and eight in diameter. Tapered towards the top and with a bulbous middle, abstractly it reminded Kane of the shape of a space hopper from his youth, a look he was determined to avoid himself as he approached what some might call middle age and the inevitable accompanying spread.

It looked to be formed in terracotta, and Kane opened the small visitor guide he'd picked up in reception to cross-reference the artefact with his guess. He was right. The humble artefact was created in approximately 1650 by an unknown artisan in the town of Arita, in the Saga Prefecture of Japan, and had become infamous when the Korean thieves had stolen it. Again, Kane marvelled at how such an innocuous object—that to an uninitiated eye might be nothing more than an ancient water urn—could be so highly prized, and in fact, considered priceless. It also boggled him that Katashi Goto wanted the thing so badly he would go to such drastic lengths, including kidnapping, to secure it.

Kane shook his head and glanced at Jae-won, who seemed to be lost in thought. Kane knew his mind wasn't on the object, but rather his son, Heung-min.

"What are you thinking?" Kane asked quietly. "You still think it's possible?"

Jae-won turned sharply to his friend… too sharply, he seemed to realise, and checked himself. He leaned in closer to Kane. "It does not matter whether I think it is possible or not possible, Hiram. We are going to leave this building with the artefact." His gaze met Kane's full on and Kane was in no doubt of Jae-won's intentions.

Kane nodded. "I understand, I do. But the question is, how? What exactly are you thinking?"

Jae-won let his gaze drift around casually, as if looking for a friend or relative there with them, but he was of course searching for cameras or security guards. Apparently seeing none—Kane hadn't spotted any either—he inhaled and led them away from that particular display case and paused at the next one, housing some other examples of earthenware.

Jae-won nodded for Kane to follow, and they ambled away from the exhibit. "There are not any guards here to my knowledge. At least, I haven't seen any. There are no cameras in this section either, that I can see, other than the one over the main entry into this hall. There might be a guard patrolling at night, but I don't really think so." Kane had to agree, now he was there.

They paused at a huge floor-to-ceiling window that afforded them a view over the vast, tranquil gardens to the rear of the museum. The museum complex was flanked to the north by the southern edge of Wolseong Forest, an area of natural beauty that like most of the ancient city, was rich in monuments and historic sites. It was also very quiet, and would be totally deserted after dark.

"My idea is to enter the complex through those trees," Jae-won said, nodding in the direction of the forest. "If we encounter any external guards, we deal with them with as little force as possible. We will only hurt them if we must. I do not think they will cause us any problem. Then we will climb to the upper level using the staff service stairs around the back of this building. I saw them when we arrived."

Kane nodded. "Yes, I saw them too. Then?"

"Then we come in through the roof." He cast a sideways glance at Kane.

Kane caught the look in his friend's eye and, although serious, he was certain he spotted at least a sliver of humour. "Like Mission Impossible?"

Jae-won didn't smile… at least not with his mouth. Nor did he frown, or grimace. The fire in his eyes though was unmistakable, as were the twitching muscles in his clenched jaw. "Not impossible," he finally muttered, and he moved away from the window.

Chapter Twenty-Five

Kane wasn't sure about Jae-won's plan. Not sure at all. He was determined to suggest they wait at least another day, to see if they could contact Katashi Goto and come to some different arrangement, some peaceful deal that might somehow appease the old gangster. He touched his friend on the shoulder. "Wait, Jae-won. Can we please discuss it a little—"

"There is nothing to discuss. I know you are going to try and talk me out of it, or at least convince me to wait. No, Hiram. There is too much at stake, and without knowing where Heung-min is I simply cannot wait until tomorrow. I *will not* wait. It is only my common sense stopping me from smashing the glass of that display case and making off with the stupid vase right now. And no, I will not involve the police…"

Jae-won let his words trail off as a woman in a museum staff uniform emerged from around the corner. For a moment it appeared she was going to approach them, but as she neared she merely paused, and offered a subtle bow of respect in their direction. Then she smiled, and was on her way.

Kane nodded. Jae-won was right. They couldn't risk involving the police, at least not yet. And they definitely could not do anything in daylight when the museum was still open to the public. That would be utter madness.

"You're right. We must wait until tonight." Kane led Jae-won by the arm and into yet another gallery, pausing at another display, this one showcasing some fine examples of embroidered Korean tapestries.

"What about alarms?" Kane said quietly. "Surely they'd be linked directly to the police station? We'd have minutes... maybe five at the most... to get out of here and away before we'd be apprehended, arrested and locked up. It's not enough time, my friend. It's too risky. There has to be another—"

"It is enough time." Jae-won grabbed Kane gently by his forearm. "Listen, I am coming back here tonight and I am leaving with the artefact. I will do it with or without your help. In fact, maybe it is better I come alone. This is not your problem. He is my son, Hiram, so maybe—"

"Not a chance," Kane said, with more energy than he'd meant. He backed off a little. "Look, Katashi Goto has taken Heung-min because of me. I am going to help you, my friend, whether you like it or not."

Jae-won exhaled through gritted teeth. He nodded slowly, eyes fixed on Kane's, and released his arm from his grasp. "I am sorry," he muttered. "I am obviously very worried. But I am pleased. Thank you, brother."

Kane held his gaze for several beats as a vague idea began to form. "How about this? We cause a disturbance somewhere else in the city. It would limit the police response at the museum. I don't know... maybe set fire to an abandoned old building somewhere on the edge of downtown? I know this bastard, Jae-won. I know Katashi Goto, and I know how he thinks. He *will* give us the time he has suggested. Just trust me on this, although I know it must be difficult to do that. He might be a hardened criminal. A violent man. A murderer, even. But despite that, I believe he has at least some honour left in his otherwise rotten soul. I have to believe that. What do you think?"

Jae-won nodded, seeming to consider Kane's words. "Yes, a distraction. I know just the place. I also know just the person to help us out. Let's get out of here now, and I will make the arrangements."

Chapter Twenty-Six

Back at the mountain-side Golgulsa temple complex, Kane left Jae-won and took himself off for a walk around the trails in the surrounding foothills. The sky was now clear and blue, and the same cool breeze that had blown the snow clouds earlier away now buffeted him from the east. He needed the fresh air, needed the space to breathe and process what they were about to do.

He paused at the western edge of a small manmade reservoir and took a seat on a rocky outcrop, tugging his insufficient jacket a little tighter around his neck. Kane was tired. He'd been sleeping well enough, at least for him, despite the nightmares and the thin and bumpy futon cot that passed for a bed in his humble digs. No, it was an innate exhaustion he felt, rather than regular tiredness. And stress. Kane was stressed.

As he peered out across the gently rippling surface of the reservoir, its dark waters brooding and ominous despite the bright sky above, he once again found himself in disbelief at the circumstances that had arisen. Of course, his main fear now was for the safety of Heung-min. The bastards also knew where Jae-won and his beloved family lived. That another innocent life or lives were potentially in peril, and that it had something to do with him, was hard for Kane to stomach.

There had been many times in the recent past when Kane found himself embroiled in such nefarious schemes… he was never the perpetrator, of course, yet he always seemed to be the common denominator. If he wasn't around, he often mused, especially when knee deep in the booze as he had been for so much of the last few months, fewer people would get hurt. Of that he was certain. He hadn't exactly considered ending it, removing himself permanently from the equation. Deep down Kane believed he still had a lot to offer the world. He at least had to believe that. But sometimes, in his lowest moments, he wondered if it wouldn't just be better for everyone if he… disappeared.

Kane stood up, then stepped down to the edge of the reservoir. He gazed at the dark surface, and imagined what it would be like beneath it.

The cold. The darkness. The silence.

The peace?

Kane exhaled slowly and closed his eyes, and was surprised Alex Ridley's face appeared in his mind. It had been many months since he'd actually seen her, and he missed her as keenly now as he did back then. In his mind's eye, Ridley was glaring at him, her face set firmly and her penetrating green eyes appraising him, almost challenging him.

Don't you dare, those eyes seemed to say. *Don't you dare even think about it…*

Kane suddenly inhaled, sucking in air to replenish the breath he hadn't realised he'd been holding. He shook his head, and Ridley disappeared from his mind. He turned away from the water and retook his seat on the rock, his attention returning to Heung-min and Jae-won, and the stolen Tripitaka Koreana. Jae-won was wrong in what he had tried to say. This *was* Kane's problem. They were his friends. Almost family. He was involved, and though not guilty, he was in some part responsible for the events that had led to Heung-min's kidnapping.

He cast his mind to the museum, and the potential hazards they faced in removing the artefact. It was risky, of course it was. They couldn't help Heung-min if they were behind bars. But maybe Jae-won was right. Maybe it wouldn't be as difficult as Kane imagined. It's true that security in South Korea was notoriously soft. Yes, there were criminals… there are criminals everywhere! But in Korea, more so than in many other Asian nations, crime rates were statistically low. Kane didn't need to be a local to know that thefts from nationally important museums were rare. So rare and unlikely, in fact, that perhaps the security systems could actually be breached without too much of a problem.

Only one way to find out, he mused as he stood up again and set himself to do some stretching. He had no idea what might transpire once they'd begun to execute their plan. Whatever it was, he wanted to be ready, both physically and mentally. As he went through his regular routine of stretches and tai-chi poses, Kane sensed he was on the cusp of a defining moment in his life. He had felt it before. It was an odd sensation, uncomfortably nestled somewhere between excitement and fear. Despite the dangers, to themselves, and of course, to Heung-min, Kane found it wasn't an altogether unpleasant sensation.

Failure was not an option, of course. To fail could result in tragic, devastating consequences for Jae-won and his family. Success, on the other hand, could set Kane free of so many demons that followed him around like a tribe of nefarious shadows. Success would mean Heung-min was safe. Success would also mean the Tripitaka was recovered, and returned, complete, to the temple complex at Haeinsa. Success would mean they had gotten the better of Katashi Goto, perhaps for the very last time.

And perhaps success might even mean Kane would have his dignity and self-worth restored. That, in the bigger picture of the other things considered, was of little significance to anyone but himself. Yet, to Kane, it was but one more reason to make sure they achieved what they needed to achieve tonight at the museum.

They would get in, and they would leave with the Vase of Heaven. They had to. There was simply no other choice.

Half an hour later Kane had made his way back up to the main square of the temple complex. From afar he could see Jae-won's wife. She appeared to be waiting for him. She wasn't smiling.

"Annyong ha-shim-nika," he called out, saying hello in the most formal, respectful way he knew. She didn't answer. Jae-won appeared from behind her, hustling over.

"The university has called. They asked about Heung-min," he said. "He never misses lectures, never, and they are worried."

"We need to call the police," his wife said sternly in her native Korean. "We must."

"No!" Jae-won said firmly, placing his hands on his wife's shoulders. More gently, he added, "We cannot do that."

Kane understood most of the words. Jae-won turned to

Kane. "Are you still okay with the plan?" he said, reverting to English.

Kane nodded. "I am. And I am ready." He motioned over his shoulder to the growing dark. Full darkness was an hour away. Kane glanced at his watch. The museum would close in an hour, at five pm. They had agreed to wait until nine that night to commence their plan.

Jae-won checked his watch too, then gazed at the sky. "My love, it is just too risky to involve the police," he said to his wife in Korean.

She shook her head and closed her eyes. To Kane it seemed as if she knew that what Jae-won was saying was right, but that she simply didn't want to believe it. She took a few moments to compose herself, inhaling deeply and letting the breath out slowly through pursed lips. She shrugged her frail shoulders out from beneath Jae-won's hands and stepped away from them both, making her way towards their small house. Kane glanced at Jae-won, whose expression ached of worry and guilt.

Then his wife turned to face them and took a step back in their direction. She cuffed a stray tear from her cheek and took a deep breath. She stared hard at her husband. Kane couldn't miss the haunted look in her narrowed eyes.

"If something happens to my Heung-min, I will forever blame you," she said to Jae-won, almost so quietly Kane had to strain to hear. Then she set her gaze upon Kane. "And you too, Hiram," she said, switching to English so as to leave zero doubt in her meaning. "I will blame you as well."

Chapter Twenty-Seven

A little before nine o'clock that evening, Jae-won pulled his car onto a grassy verge along the deserted minor road to the south of Wolsong Forest,. It was very near the refurbished eighth century Woljeong Bridge, that had long ago served as the only crossing of the moat that surrounded the ancient Banwolseong Fort, which once stood on the land. Gentle flurries of snow drifted in the beams of the car's headlights.

Jay-won killed the engine, plunging the area into near total darkness. The two of them sat there in silence for a moment, letting their eyes adjust to the conditions. With the car's heater now off, the cold quickly let itself be known.

Finally Kane spoke. "What's so special about that vase, anyway? I mean, I understand all artefacts are important culturally. But that one? Well, it looks so... ordinary." Whether he was genuinely interested, or whether it was a delaying tactic, Kane himself wasn't sure.

"It might only be a humble piece of history to you and I, but it is special to *them*." He shot a sideways glance at Kane, who nodded at the emphasis of Jae-won's final word.

"The Japanese?"

Jae-won huffed. "It was stolen from *them* by Koreans back in the nineteenth century. Despite what we think of it, some scholars believe it is worth more than ten billion Korean won."

Kane did a quick mental calculation in his mind. "Holy shit… that's about six million pounds… almost eight million dollars. That's… well, right, no wonder he—"

"It is only money, Hiram! He has my son…"

Kane fell silent again. Jae-won was right. It was only money. He wondered about Katashi Goto's real intentions. Surely it couldn't only be about the money. The man had been rich for decades. He doubted those vast reserves of wealth had been depleted in the few short years since he'd been incarcerated. Especially since he was officially dead.

Perhaps pretending to be dead is expensive? It was an amusing thought. Kane didn't smile.

"So if we manage to get this thing," he said, turning to face his friend, "do you really believe Katashi will trade it for Heung-min, as well as returning the stolen blocks of the Tripitaka?"

Jae-won didn't answer for long moments, as if trying to decide what he really believed. Through the windscreen a layer of snow had built up on the car's bonnet. Jae-won closed his eyes, inhaling deeply of the frigid air, before letting it out slowly. "I have to believe that. I have to. It seems as if the bastard does not value life as much as he does material wealth. Yes, Hiram… I believe he will return Heung-min to us."

Kane considered this. *Do I believe that? The man is a psycho.* Kane realised he wasn't sure. One thing that was sure, was that they would find out soon enough. "Are you ready, my friend?" he asked. Jae-won nodded.

Despite the gloom enshrouding them, Kane could see well enough to not miss the look of grim determination in his friend's eyes. Kane nodded back, then turned and opened the car door. As he was half way out, Jae-won grabbed him firmly by the forearm.

"Because if he does not, I will hunt him down, and I will kill him."

Chapter Twenty-Eight

Heung-min jolted awake. He'd been dreaming... of galbi and pajeon, and washing them down with beer and soju with his friends. He heard his stomach grumble in the darkness as he shifted position.

He kept his eyes closed when he heard the now familiar creak of the door's hinges as it swung open. The person that visited daily to bring food and water was almost always the same; a woman, whom he guessed to be somewhere in her late twenties, perhaps thirties based on her voice. He hadn't yet seen her face. She never turned the light on until she was almost out of the room. She had never said more than a half dozen words to him, though he had tried to engage her constantly. He'd seen the movies. There was always one kidnapper in the group with a conscience. As yet, he didn't believe it to be this woman. Still, Heung-min wasn't about to give up.

"Why are you doing this?" he asked, though he expected to receive the same answer she'd already given several times. "Why are you keeping me here, locked up in the dark like a rabid dog?"

"I told you already," she said, her monotone demonstrating her apparent indifference to his plight, "it is just a job."

"What job?" Heung-min persisted. "All you do is bring me food. It does not seem like much of a job." He wasn't trying to antagonise her... not really. Still, he knew it was a risk.

The woman didn't say anything for a long moment, and Heung-min wondered if she was deciding between answering him or kicking him in the teeth. He didn't have to wait long to find out.

Her foot swung at him so hard that it was out of control and instead of finding its intended target, it glanced off his solid left shoulder and missed his head altogether. The momentum of the swing sent her foot crashing into the wall and threw her off balance, and like a coiled tiger, Heung-min sprung to his knees and threw himself over her, pinning her down with his considerable weight. With his one free hand, he grappled for her mouth and clamped down, muffling her attempts at a scream for help.

Beneath his body he felt her struggle, and although game, she was no match for his strength. He let his weight pin her down, waiting until her struggles became subdued, which didn't take long. After a minute of stillness, he spoke to her quietly. "Please listen to me. I do not know who you are. I am not going to hurt you. As you said, you are just doing your job. Why will you not help me? I am only nineteen. Whatever this is... whoever you are working for... I am sure it is all a mistake. I am young, still a student... what do they want with me? Please, help me..."

The woman remained silent for long moments, until

finally Heung-min heard the faintest of sobs. The woman's shoulders—Heung-min now realised she was very lean, almost frail—began to shudder, as if she were suddenly afraid. *Good!*

"It is okay. I promise I will not hurt you," he said quietly. "I understand you are only doing what they make you do. And I will not ask anything too difficult of you. I do not want you to get in trouble."

The woman's shoulders fell still and her sobs ceased. Heung-min gently eased his hand away from her mouth, but kept it close. "Please do not scream or yell. That will be bad for both of us." The woman nodded that she understood. "All I ask of you is this… First, where are we? And second, if it were possible, would you get a message out of the building for me? My parents will be very worried. I just want to let them know I am okay."

The woman's breathing had slowed to a near-normal rate, and she seemed to relax somewhat. Heung-min eased himself off her, shifting his weight to the side and kneeling next to her, allowing her the space to turn onto her back. He kept himself poised though, one hand near her mouth. Just in case.

Slowly and carefully, the woman turned over and rested back on her elbows. She had a graze on her forehead where she'd been pressed against the floor, and her eyes were puffy from the tears.

"I am sorry about your head," Heung-min said, nodding at the minor injury. "You did try to kick me in mine," he reminded her, and against his better judgment, he offered her a smile.

The woman didn't return the smile, but her stoic face did soften visibly. "I am sorry too."

"Listen, we do not have much time. I am sure you need

to get back downstairs before they get suspicious. Whoever they are. So, will you help me?"

The woman—who Heung-min now saw was barely older than him—swallowed hard, clearly torn. "I… I do not know…"

"I promise, if you help me, I will help you too when the time comes. No one needs to know what you have done. Just take a simple message, and send it to my family. Tell them I am okay. Tell them where I am. Can you help me? Will you do it?"

The young woman sat up straighter, then rose to her knees and closed her eyes. "What is your name?" she asked, still not looking.

The fact she didn't know his name made it seem to Heung-min that she really was just a small cog in this operation. She was probably being forced into it against her will, and she may yet prove to be a useful ally. He didn't want to force the issue, but he had to seize his moment.

"My name is Heung-min," he told her. "What is your name?"

Finally, the woman opened her eyes and looked at him, her stoic facade all but evaporated. "My name… my name is Mika. Yes, I will help you."

Chapter Twenty-Nine

The two men trotted through the light snow and heavy darkness along the deserted road until they reached the ancient bridge. Jae-won had explained that the bridge once served as the only entrance to the fort that guarded the palace that had stood there two thousand years ago, but was now just a series of ruins. It had been a different age and a different time, and Kane wondered abstractedly if it were a better age and a better time. He suspected it probably was.

They made it across Woljeong Bridge, and headed east several hundred yards, clinging to the curving edge of the river until they entered the menacing darkness of Wolseong Forest where they slowed to catch their breath. It was just a further hundred yards to the edge of the forest, which stood opposite the Gyeongju National Museum.

"Are you sure you want to do this?" Jae-won quietly asked Kane. "It is not your fight, my friend."

Kane turned to face his mentor. "Yes!" he stated plainly. "I am with you, whatever it takes."

"You know," Jae-won said, a hint of warning in his tone, "there is a high chance innocent people are going to get hurt tonight. Are you prepared for that? Do you want that blood... *more* blood on your hands?"

Kane stared at Jae-won, then let his eyes drift off into the pitch-black of the forest canopy above. After long, silent moments, his gaze lowered back to his friend's, and then settled on his own hands, resting in his lap. Kane hadn't missed the implications of Jae-won's warning. He'd seen a lot of blood in recent times, that was true. Some of it was down to Kane himself. "Yes, I understand. I am prepared to do what I can to help you get your son back. We agreed, violence as a last resort. Right?"

Jae-won nodded. "Right. I do not think it will come to that. Yet, any Korean parent would do the same. They would understand. Nevertheless, I am sure we can deal with any security guards effectively and without violence, as long as we are careful. But... I *will* do what I need to do, Hiram... I need you to understand that!"

Kane returned the nod. He did understand... if it were his son, he would feel the same. In fact, it wasn't his son and yet he felt the same anyway.

"From now on, no speaking. There is no need. Follow my lead, and stay alert. Good?"

"Good." Kane nodded once more, both to show his acquiescence and to fortify his own belief. "Ka-ja," he added in Korean. *Let's go.*

Both men pulled on the black balaclavas they'd brought with them and then they set off.

Kane followed Jae-won cautiously down the forested slope to the road that dissected the forest and the museum complex. The quiet, empty road was edged by a high fence on the opposite side, which they would have to scale in due course. They didn't think there would be CCTV or any alarms involved at this stage.

Glancing right, Kane saw that the river formed the eastern boundary of the complex, and he nodded in that direction. Jae-won understood the implication, and the two men darted towards the road bridge, ducked beneath the bridge on the river's bank, and emerged the other side, just outside the fence in a secluded corner of the museum. Less than a minute later, both men were safely up and over the fence and within the museum's grounds.

Without pause, Jae-won hustled south along the inner side of the fence until they came parallel with the Su-mug-dang building, one of the main museum galleries. It was not the one they needed to access. Using that building as cover, they then hurried around the back of that structure towards the primary museum building, on the northern quadrant of the main central courtyard.

Here they paused again, and took a moment to breathe and listen for any motion around them. After a full two minutes, and confident their activities remained unknown, Jae-won turned to face Kane. Silently, he motioned with his hand to the service stairs that clung to the rear of the building and led all the way to the roof, with two mezzanine landings with doors to each floor of the museum a third and then two-thirds of the way up. Jae-won pointed all the way to the top, and nodded. Kane returned the nod, and seconds later they were scurrying up those stairs to the roof, each gentle thud of their feet on the metal stairs reverberating like thunder in Kane's ears.

Once at the top they paused again and Jae-won glanced around, nervously scanning the ground below for any sign of security. Kane joined in the search. For a moment it seemed as if the entire place was deserted, then Kane spotted what appeared to be the beam of a flashlight bobbing along where he believed the western perimeter fence was.

Dammit, he thought… *not alone after all.*

Jae-won had seen it too but didn't seem to be affected by it. It didn't change anything. They were going in. Around the rim of the building, beneath the eaves of the roof, there stretched a narrow walkway, wide enough for one person to access it for service purposes. Jae-won had known this from studying the building's architectural plans online that afternoon. He was prepared for it, and began to make his way cautiously along the edge to where he knew a door was set into the wall. Behind that wall, he knew, was the room that housed the high-tech air-conditioning units used to moderate the temperature within the museum and to protect the exhibits. That was to be their access point.

Moments later they'd arrived. Then, from a small backpack he was wearing Jae-won retrieved a set of skeleton keys. Kane was surprised, but assumed—and hoped—one of them would open the door without the need for force.

Kane shot Jae-won a questioning glance when he saw the keys… he hadn't known about this, but was relieved. He'd been expecting a more agricultural approach to gaining entry inside. Jae-won returned Kane's glance with a nervous one of his own. This wasn't him… not his character at all. Kane knew the most illegal thing Jae-won had ever done before was drive through a red light. He'd even been pulled over by a bored policeman. However, when the young officer saw the driver was his senior by at least a decade, he apparently offered a little bow, and backed off, waving Jae-won on his way. Sometimes, Jae-won had thought at the time, and later shared with Kane, the rules and traditions of Confucianism had their benefits.

But it was to both Jae-won's and Kane's relief when the second key Jae-won tried in the simple lock yielded without protest, and the door swung silently open. They shared a quick glance, then stepped through.

They were in.

Chapter Thirty

Entry into the building had been easier than both men had truly expected. Despite the knowledge that security in Korea perhaps wasn't as good as it should be, they'd still deep down both expected some form of resistance, whether that be electronically via alarms or sensor systems, or by baton-wielding night watchmen. Neither had materialised. Yet.

That didn't mean they were home and dry. Not even close.

Jae-won glanced at his watch. The hint of a grin glinted in his eyes.

"What is it?" Kane asked, seeing his friend's apparent amusement.

"Ten o'clock."

"What about it?" Kane whispered.

"That abandoned old market building downtown I mentioned. It is going to be demolished next month… we are giving them a head start. It is about to burn to the ground. Come on," he whispered through his balaclava.

Jae-won led them through the sizeable room that housed the gallery's high-tech climate control systems, and paused at the door which presumably led them into the upper gallery itself. The old friends shared an encouraging nod. Jae-won tried the door. Predictably, they found it locked. Jae-won once again took the skeleton keys from his pocket and set about trying one after another in the lock. This time they weren't so lucky. After trying each of the dozen or so keys twice, the lock had failed to yield. They would have to gain access by force.

In his early forties, Kane was a decade and a half younger than his former tae-kwon-do guru, and physically fitter, perhaps stronger too. However, despite Kane being highly skilled in the Korean martial art, Jae-won was still the master.

"Allow me," he whispered, though his pinched brow betrayed his lack of confidence. Getting through the door wasn't the issue. Not letting any security guards who might be lurking somewhere behind know of their illegal presence was.

Jae-won took a step back from the door and paused a moment to compose himself. The door didn't appear especially sturdy, but it was likely set with alarms. Not to stop people getting out... but to stop nosy gallery-goers from getting in.

With a burst of power, Jae-won slammed his boot against the door just below the lock. A hefty thud resounded back at them, but not much else happened. He repeated the motion, this time emitting a determined grunt. His booted foot made contact in the exact same spot as before, and this time left a significant dent in the door. The lock remained steadfast.

"One more should do it," Kane whispered, though

whispering now seemed futile. If there were any guards anywhere near that room, they would have surely heard the loud thuds coming from within.

Jae-won nodded. There was nothing left to do but to just go for it. He stepped back once more, took a deep breath and smashed his foot twice in rapid succession into the same location. This time the lock broke away from the door as it swung open, crashing into the wall outside the room before slowly swinging back closed. Kane moved quickly and grabbed the door, easing it to a stop. Both men automatically ducked low behind the doorframe, listening for any sign of alarm or concerned voices. Somewhat surprisingly, Kane heard nothing other than the sound of his own pulse in his ears.

The two men shared a nervous glance. Then, after several seconds of silence, Jae-won's eyebrows rose, his eyes crinkling into the faintest of smiles, as if to say, *We are in.*

Kane nodded, and stood, peering out through the narrow crack between the door and its frame. Beyond the room they were currently in he saw a vast gallery spreading out before him, with lines of exhibits in glass cases on either side of a wide corridor. Delicate lighting cast long, motionless shadows about the floor. Otherwise, all was still and quiet. No security guards in sight. He nodded at Jae-won and the two of them cautiously left the sanctuary of the climate control room and, hugging the wall, Jae-won led them along that first corridor, making a beeline towards the next gallery, where he knew their prize awaited.

Just outside the huge open-plan atrium-style building, twenty-year-old Nam-gil stomped out his cigarette beneath his job-supplied black boots and scanned his security ID against the digital unit on the wall. A beep sounded as a hidden lock disengaged. He pushed open the door and stepped into the foyer of the main gallery. Nam-gil glanced around the vast space and huffed.

Shit, this posting is so boring.

Like all young Korean men, Nam-gil had to complete his mandatory military service. This was his first year, and as was standard, he had been tasked with what was considered a safe, and easy, yet worthwhile public service. That's not how Nam-gil considered it. Some of his friends had become part-time police officers or firemen. Others were traffic wardens, or worked as security on the country's super-sleek metro systems. Those were the kind of postings he wanted, where there might be some excitement, or where he could at least gaze at young Korean women on the subway all day. Anything but being stuck here on the nightshift of an empty, dreary museum where the only action was watching baseball on his mobile phone when he went out for a smoke, which he found himself doing far too often.

I wish we were at war with the North... that would be much more interesting.

He didn't mean it of course. Still...

Nam-gil didn't even have anyone to talk to while on duty, and he'd already called his girlfriend twice. There was the older security guard who was currently on perimeter duty somewhere outside, and he was so old Nam-gil wondered if he should be an exhibit in the museum rather than being paid to wander around outside it.

Who is the old bastard guarding the museum from anyway? Nam-gil mused, grinning wryly. *Fucking squirrels? Ah, Hyo-jin... if only you were here, we could mess around in the office—*

Dummph!

Nam-gil paused mid-stride as he thought he heard something from somewhere on one of the upper levels.

Dummph!

There it was again; a dull thud, like someone bouncing an oversized basketball.

Then again, twice in rapid succession, and Nam-gil felt his fingertips buzz with electricity as adrenaline coursed through his system.

What the…?

Without thinking, Nam-gil raced over to the stairs and then thought better of it, slowing down and then pausing to think and listen. Everything had fallen silent, and the thudding, whatever it was, had ceased.

Did I imagine it? he wondered, though he felt certain he hadn't. He plucked the walkie talkie from his waist belt and hit the Speak button. "Seok-ho, are you there?" he said into the device. It was the first time he'd ever used it. "Seok-ho?" he said again, his voice a harsh whisper.

"Mua?" came the flat reply. The old man's voice quiet and he sounded uninterested. *What?*

"I think there is a… I think maybe there is someone in the museum."

"Nonsense, boy," Seok-ho said dismissively. "Impossible. It is only your cowardly imagination."

"No, sir," Nam-gil persisted, this time more politely so as to get the old man's attention. "I heard some banging upstairs. I think… it sounded like a door being forced open. I think you should come inside."

There followed a long silence, too long, Nam-gil thought, before Seok-ho finally grunted into the device. "Okay. Stay where you are. I will be five minutes."

Nam-gil nodded to himself and clipped the device back onto his belt. His heart hammered and he heard rather than felt the blood pounding through his ears. The old man had told him to stay where he was. Protocol dictated that is what he should do, both in his employment training's rules, and in the largely adhered to culture of Confucianism. Yet Nam-gil had been crying out for something to disrupt the monotony of the job. Perhaps this was it…

He started to make his way slowly up the stairs to the second level. The security guards of the museum were armed. All were permitted to carry a small firearm, though never in a million years did Nam-gil ever expect to have to use it. Nevertheless, he unholstered the gun now, checked the safety was on and held it carefully out in front of him as he slowly ascended the stairs, wondering with a grin if squirrels in fact could really break into a museum.

Chapter Thirty-One

Kane felt his confidence grow as they hustled along the wide corridor, sticking to the right-hand wall and staying out of view as best they could. They had neither seen nor heard any sign of actual security guards inside the building, and other than the bobbing torch on the perimeter fence suggesting at least one exterior guard, all seemed quiet on that front. They did know there were security cameras dotted around, but whether they were even live was unknown… they just had to assume they were, and they stayed out of sight of their roving lenses as much as was possible. So far so good.

"It is just through that entrance to the next gallery," Jae-won whispered to Kane as he pulled them into a crouch behind a large glass display cabinet housing a collection of porcelain artefacts. Just thirty yards ahead, a wide gap in the facing wall, flanked by two impressive carved statues of what Kane recognised as Silla-era warriors, led through to the gallery that was home to the artefact they were there to steal.

Does it count as stealing, if it is for such an important cause? Kane mused abstractedly, and supposed that in fact it did, regardless of their justifiable reasons. It mattered little what name you gave it. They were about to 'remove' a priceless artefact from a museum... without permission. It was theft, plain and simple.

They were just about to move on into the next gallery when Jae-won suddenly paused again. His eyes flashed to Kane as he reached into his pocket to retrieve his mobile phone. Jae-won had earlier instructed his wife to only message if it was with news about Heung-min. Kane knew it might even be Heung-min himself, and understood his friend had to check his messages.

Kane watched Jae-won's eyes as they scanned the text. His expression was unreadable beneath the balaclava, until at last a hint of emotion flickered in his eyes and he turned to Kane.

"What is it?" Kane whispered. "Is it Heung-min?"

The barest trace of a smile glinted in his eyes as an even smaller suggestion of a grin curled one corner of Jae-won's lip, just visible through a gap in the black material. He nodded, so subtly Kane hardly registered it. "Yes," he whispered. "It's Ju-hye... she has received word from an unknown source saying they have spoken to Heung-min. She was told that our son is okay."

Kane held in his joy for a moment. It sounded good news, but who the hell was it? "Who is the messenger, Jae-won? How can you be sure it is genuine?"

"I... I feel it is true," Jae-won said so quietly Kane had to lean in closer to hear. "My wife says the text she received was from a withheld number. There was also a location."

"Really? The place where Heung-min is being held? In Daegu?"

Jae-won nodded. "Yes, an address in the industrial district north of the downtown area."

Kane knew the city... South Korea's fourth largest. Why Katashi Goto would hold Heung-min there he had no idea. "So what do we do? Are we still going to get the object?" Kane whispered, motioning with his head towards the other gallery.

"Yes, we must still get the artefact. And we must get it now!"

With that, Jae-won rose and started off at a trot into the other gallery.

Nam-gil had ascended the first flight of stairs to the middle gallery and surveilled the area quickly. He'd paused to listen, and though uncertain, he thought he might have heard noise coming from the upper tier of the museum. Having seen no trace of any presence on the middle floor, he hustled back to the stairs and made his way swiftly but silently to the top level. There he paused again, wondering how long it would take the old bastard to join him from outside.

Nam-gil then walked with purpose, gun still held out front, along the eastern flank of the top floor, which is when he spotted the door to the climate control room hanging open. He ran over to it, gun aloft and heart racing, and stopped ten feet short. He felt his heartbeat tick up another level. He listened, but heard nothing. Now certain one or more intruders had gained illegal access to the museum, Nam-gil went on high alert. Shit was getting real.

Kane followed swiftly after Jae-won, certain it was foolish to abandon their tactic of keeping a low profile.

"Jae-won," he hissed in a harsh whisper. "Jae-won, wait... we must be careful."

Jae-won had either not heard Kane or had blatantly ignored him as his pace didn't slow, and he jogged on through the wide entranceway past the two inanimate stone guards towards their quarry, which lie in wait around two more corners of the upper tier and still out of sight.

Shit! Kane was worried Jae-won was going to blow their own cover before they even had a chance to retrieve the item in question. He followed on anyway, sure they were in too deep to turn back. Knowing the man as he did, for over two decades, he knew his friend was as stubborn as he was wise and strong. Getting the alleged confirmation his son was okay was clearly driving Jae-won now, even if Kane had some reservations about the message his wife had sent. Either way, it had clearly inspired Jae-won to get the artefact and get out of there as soon as possible. It was making him reckless.

They slowed only marginally as they approached the penultimate corner and were now racing along the northern side of the building, slowing again only as they approached the final turn. Kane grabbed Jae-won by the shoulder and stepped in front of his friend.

"We must be careful," Kane said harshly yet quietly. He looked into Jae-won's eyes through the openings in the balaclava and saw a fierce determination there. Jae-won blinked a couple of times, as if coming to some realisation.

"I know... you are right. Careful..." Jae-won shook his head, inhaling deeply. "But they have my son." With that, Jae-won unceremoniously shoved his old friend out of the way and rushed towards the final corner, which he turned before coming to a jolting, juddering stop.

"Jeong-ji! I-dong-ha-ji an-seub-nida!" yelled the security guard that now stood between Jae-won and the artefact. *Halt. Do not move, or I will shoot!*

Chapter Thirty-Two

Oh shit. Oh shit, shit, shit!!

Kane skidded to an abrupt halt, crashing into the back of Jae-won who had inexplicably stopped too. Momentum had toppled Kane over the stumbling Jae-won and the pair of them had landed in a heap on the cool, smooth tiled floor of the gallery.

As Kane looked up, momentarily disoriented, he found himself staring into the business end of a gun.

He recoiled instinctively, but when the security guard, who looked no more than about fifteen to Kane's eyes, didn't move, and in fact appeared to be more shocked than he himself felt, he held still. Jae-won cast him an anxious glance, but neither man moved for several beats.

The tension in the air was palpable as silence fell heavily over the gallery. Kane noticed Jae-won's chest rising and falling as his breathing intensified, but Kane sensed it wasn't out of fear. He also noticed his friend's jowls clenching, as if he was deciding on something. Kane then watched as Jae-won closed his eyes and slowly exhaled, the sound of his purged breath loud in the silence.

Then Jae-won's eyes shot open and with the grace of an experienced cat, he sprang to his feet and took a step towards the young guard.

"Me-om chuh-weo!" the guard declared. *Stop!*

The guard took an involuntary step back but kept his eyes fixed on Jae-won's and his gun aimed somewhere towards his chest.

"No, Jae-won!" Kane said. "Stop…"

Jae-won again ignored his friend and took another step forwards, to which the guard retreated a step to match it.

"Let me through," Jae-won said in their native Korean, his voice calm and quiet. "There does not need to be any trouble."

"Ah-neh-yo!" the guard retorted, his voice anything but calm. *No!*

"Listen, kid, let me through and there will be no trouble. I know you are merely doing your duty. Your military service?" The young man said nothing, though Jae-won was sure. "I am grateful for that. But I am coming past you now and I recommend you put the gun down."

To Kane, the guard's eyes seemed to gloss over a little, as if the entire scenario was too much for him to handle. Kane again thought he looked too young to be in this position, perhaps twenty years old upon closer inspection. But under pressure like this, who knew how a young man might react. Jae-won was taking a huge yet calculated risk.

"Let me through, son," he said again. "You do not know what you are doing by impeding me this way."

"I can… I cannot let you past. It is my duty. You should not be here."

Jae-won turned to look at Kane. Kane saw in his friend's

eyes inner conflict, and turmoil was written across his face in deep lines. There was some empathy there for the young guard who was only doing his job. Yet there was one more emotion he saw there. It registered in a slight narrowing of the eyes. In the steely glint that arrowed from them. In the way his jaw clenched…

"Please, sir, do not make me have to shoot you," the guard pleaded, his voice now thick with emotion.

"I warned you!" Jae-won grunted.

"No!" Kane yelled, but it was too late. Jae-won accelerated fast, like a sprinter off the blocks and belying his fifty plus years.

The gunshot that took him down sounded like a huge balloon popping next to Kane's ear. As if in slow motion, Jae-won's left leg crumpled beneath him and he fell heavily to the tiles. The man roared like a wounded lion. Kane saw the young guard standing stock-still, as if frozen on the spot. His face had screwed up in horror. He lowered the gun, and his eyes drifted down with it, as if forgetting it was even there.

It was then Kane realised he hadn't actually fired.

"Do not move," came another voice from just behind Kane. The words were in English, but heavily accented. "I will do what I have to do to protect my museum."

Kane angled his head to the right and saw who had spoken the words. A second security guard stood there, as calm as if he were collecting money for tickets at the entrance. Only the flint-like gaze in his eyes suggested there was a serious situation developing.

Kane nodded. He didn't move. This guard clearly meant business. He flicked his gaze to Jae-won, who had crawled a couple of yards to his left and now sat leaning against a display cabinet, his shot leg splayed out before him and blood pooling around his calf muscle in a dark puddle. Jae-won's gaze found Kane and what Kane saw there was not what he'd expected. Rather than agonised torment—surely his friend was in tremendous pain—he saw fear and worry, not for himself, Kane knew, but for his son and for his inability to help him from this moment forth.

The young guard had seen enough, and despite this being his military duty, he placed his gun on the floor. Kane imagined what must be going through his mind. Shock. Doubt. Fear. Perhaps a sense of failing in his duty. Kane couldn't blame him and wasn't surprised when he bowed towards the older guard, mumbled an apology, then turned on his heels and fled. Kane believed he would be of no further threat, though he would almost certainly raise the alarm.

Kane was torn. He knew any chance of success had now landed squarely on his shoulders. Jae-won's injured leg would need treating too, and there was clearly no way he could continue.

Kane turned slowly towards the guard. In his best Korean, he said, "This has been a simple mistake. We are no threat to you, sir. Please, lower your gun."

The older security guard—Jeong-sil Woo, according to his name tag—remained stoic, unmoving despite the drama. He narrowed his eyes at Kane, and Kane sensed he was being appraised for any genuine threat.

He must have thought it was real if he shot Jae-won, Kane supposed.

Kane would have to be careful. He turned back to his friend, whose face he realised now exhibited clear signs of agony. Kane knew the initial shock of being shot out of the blue must have worn off.

"My friend, it will be okay," he said in English,

suspecting the old guard understood well enough. "I will take care of things. You need to take care of yourself, now... understand?"

"Stop talking!" The old guard jabbed Kane in the back with his gun.

"Do you understand me?" Kane persisted to Jae-won. He had to make sure his friend did.

Slowly, realisation dawned on Jae-won's face. His expression was one of gratitude as well as sad resignation that he himself had failed. Kane pitied his friend, but was ready to take on the mission alone. Kane nodded at Jae-won.

Jae-won returned it and then let his eyes drift towards the older security guard, who remained motionless and stoic. In his most passive voice, Jae-won said, "I am sorry, sir. It has all been a mistake. I... we were—"

Kane swung so fast, that the security guard named Jeong-sil had half a second to react. It was nowhere near enough. Kane's left fist slammed into his throat, causing Jeong-sil to emit a spluttering growl. Kane followed up with a right cross to the temple, wobbling the man on his feet. In a flash Kane sent out a stunning straight-legged kick at the guard's gun hand, though the old man was stubborn, and strong enough not to relinquish his grip on the weapon.

With surprising fortitude, he shrugged away from Kane and stepped a couple of yards back, raising the gun once more and pointing it directly at Kane's head.

"Do not test me, way-gook-in!" he stated calmly, using the generic Korean word for foreigner, and Kane thought he was remaining almost scarily calm under the circumstances.

Shit! What now?

Kane raised his hands in an effort to pacify the guard,

who kept his steely gaze fixed on the intruder to his museum, for that's how Kane sensed he considered it—*his* museum—when on shift. *An admirable quality,* Kane mused.

"Like I said, there has been a misunderstanding," Kane told him. "My friend's son, some bad men… well, his son has been kidnapped. We just want to get him back." Kane noticed the tiniest hint of doubt creep into the old man's eyes. As the guard angled his gaze to Jae-won, Kane noticed a flash of movement over the guard's shoulder. It was the kid… who'd apparently had a change of heart.

"Stop!" the young guard yelled as he sprinted down the gallery. "Stop!"

This time Kane didn't hold back, using the distraction to launch a roundhouse kick to the guard's head before he could react. It crumpled the man where he stood and the gun dropped from his hand as he fell, and bounced across the ground and landed within reach of Jae-won, who grabbed the weapon just in time to aim it at the kid as he came to a skidding halt twenty yards short of their position.

"Son, you would be wise to back away," Jae-won told him in Korean, gently but with authority.

Kane saw the guard's bravado diminish before his eyes, apparently almost as quickly as it had returned. The young man lowered the gun, placed it on the floor and dropped to his knees with his hands up.

Kane glanced at Jae-won. "Are you okay? Can you walk?"

Jae-won almost smiled. Almost. "No, Hiram, I cannot walk. But do not worry about me. I will be okay. You must take the artefact. Take the Vase of Heaven, and go and get Heung-min. Do you hear me?"

Kane nodded. Again, he was torn. He knew what he needed to do, but he didn't like the idea of leaving his friend here injured and at the mercy of the police. He didn't like it one bit.

Then his mind inadvertently drifted to his grandfather, Hiram Snr, and as he often did in moments of adversity and indecision, Kane asked himself what his grandfather would do. The question was not easy, yet the answer was. He would do what his friend wanted, and get the object they had come for. Then he would get the hell out of there.

Kane nodded at his friend. Jae-won smiled faintly. Then, wincing in pain, he grunted and said, "Go. Please. For my son!"

Kane glanced down at the stricken older guard. He was rousing from being knocked out. Kane didn't want to hurt the man any more than was necessary, especially since he was only doing his duty. However, there was no time for sentiment. He knelt down by the man's side and, using a trick he'd learned from Jae-won two decades earlier, one that involved sensitive pressure points in the neck, he dug his fingers in and the man stopped moving instantly.

Kane glanced once more at Jae-won, whose eyes never left the young guard, who now sat passively on the floor to the right of the gallery's central aisle.

There were no more words needed between Kane and Jae-won. Ke nodded once, and then set off at a run along the gallery.

Chapter Thirty-Three

"Wait!" Jae-won yelled, his voice panicked. "Hiram, wait!"

For Jae-won to be calling him back now meant it must be serious. Kane ceased his run towards the artefact and trotted back to his friend, glancing at the young guard as he passed. The guard stared at him, his expression neutral. Kane ignored him and approached Jae-won.

"What is it?" Kane asked, noticing the concern darkening his friend's eyes.

"I got a message… a video. It is from him!"

"Katashi? Shit What's it of?"

Jae-won swallowed and played the short video. The two men looked on in horror as the video showed a man, on the ground and attempting to defend himself, being kicked by at least two pairs of black boots. Kane heard audible thuds and grunts as the boots landed with sickening power into the hunched up body, assaulting the man's back, his sides and his torso. Kane glanced at Jae-won, whose wide-eyed glare didn't leave the small screen once. Kane noticed his friend's nostrils flaring. After around twenty seconds of relentless assault, the kicks stopped and the body was rolled over. A hood was yanked off the man's head; the face was now clear to see in the video.

"Holy shit," Kane muttered, his throat suddenly dry. It was Heung-min. His face was bloodied and bruised, and his nose appeared to be broken.

Jae-won then roared, and it reverberated around the upper gallery.

Kane glanced back at the screen, that was now blank, though the video was still running.

"Your time is running out," came a voice that was frighteningly calm. It was also unmistakable.

"Katashi Goto," Kane stated. The video then ended.

Jae-won inhaled deeply and cuffed a stray tear from his cheek. He hit the call button on the phone. The dial tone sounded only twice before the call was answered.

"Do you have my artefact yet?"

Jae-won inhaled, his eyes narrowing as he fought to control his burgeoning rage. "We need more time. Just another two hours, maybe three."

A long silence followed, before Katashi finally answered. "Two hours. Two more hours, or the boy dies."

Kane heard Katashi's now familiar chuckling, then it faded, as Katashi presumably moved the phone away from his face.

"It is not enough time," Jae-won barked, but Katashi had cut the call.

Kane then turned and hustled over to the young guard. His security badge told him his name was Nam-gil.

"Nam-gil?" Kane confirmed. The young man, his eyes now wide, nodded. "Nam-gil, did you call the police? Did you raise the alarm and send any warning to anyone?"

Nam-gil shook his head. Kane searched the guard's

eyes, appraising him for his integrity. Nam-gil blinked under the scrutiny. Kane sensed he was telling the truth.

"Sir, I did not call police," he said in passable English. "Jin-jai-yo," he added, which Kane knew meant *Really* in English. Kane believed him.

"Do you know what is happening here?" Kane asked him.

"I think so. Yes. Ama-do," he said. *Maybe.*

"Then why didn't you call the police?"

"I… I do not know," Nam-gil said. "Please, sir. I can help you."

Jae-won yelled over. "Hiram, what is he saying?"

Kane turned to Nam-gil. "Why? How can we trust you?"

Nam-gil squinted, trying to recall what those English words meant.

Jae-won called out the translation. Nam-gil nodded. "I do not like Jeong-sil. He is… Ja-ji." Kane frowned.

Again, Jae-won translated. "Prick," he said dispassionately.

"Listen, Nam-gil. I am going to take something from this gallery I should not take. Okay?"

Nam-gil nodded.

"Then I must leave. Will you help my friend to get out of here? I want you to help him escape. He needs medical attention."

Jae-won translated in rapid-fire Korean. Nam-gil's eyes lit up in comprehension. Jae-won added in Korean, "It is the best military service you could do. One day, when this is all over, I promise you your superiors will understand."

Nam-gil nodded and turned back to Kane. "Yes, sir. I understand. You can… trust? You can trust me."

Kane inhaled, studying the kid's eyes for any hint of

dishonesty. Again, he found none there. "Okay," he said. "I have to go. Please help my friend out of here. Okay?"

"Okay." Nam-gil nodded and Kane watched as he stood up and cautiously approached Jae-won, apparently still wary of what these men were capable of.

Kane understood the young man's caution. They *had* just boken into a museum and assaulted an aging guard. Kane looked down at the old man, still curled up on the floor. He wouldn't be troubling anyone anytime soon.

He went to Jae-won and took his hand. "I will go now. Let this kid help you get out of here, okay? And you can trust me too, Jae-won. I will not let you down."

Kane and Nam-gil helped pull Jae-won up onto his feet. Kane saw Jae-won gritting his teeth against a wave of obvious pain and he thought his friend was going to throw up, but he swallowed down the evident agony and rose to his full height.

He clasped Kane by his shoulders. "I know you will not fail," Jae-won said through the pain, which showed clearly in his squinting eyes. Then those eyes widened as the grip on Kane's shoulders tightened. "You can not."

Kane nodded, and then he was gone.

In downtown Gyeongju, what had started as a small fire in the basement of an abandoned market building had quickly developed into a conflagration. The decrepit wood-framed structure, which sprawled from the banks of the Nam-chon river to the west and reached the boundary of Dong-guk University to the south, had soon succumbed to the inferno. With minimal threat to any of the surrounding buildings, the man who had started the fire with a couple of tins of gasoline and a discarded cigarette calmly watched on from the trees by the river as at least half a dozen fire engines raced to the scene, accompanied by several ambulances and, more importantly, seven or eight police cars. The man grinned. That many police cars would contain almost all the active on-duty police officers in this tranquil, almost backwater of a city. He knew the ambulances wouldn't be needed. The old market had been derelict for a decade and officially declared condemned for most of that time. Not even wayward kids ventured there anymore. *The local council should probably give me a medal,* he mused.

Then, lighting another cigarette, the man strode off along the river, happy to have done his old friend Jae-won a favour.

Chapter Thirty-Four

There was nothing else for it now. Kane knew he simply had to do whatever he could to remove the artefact from the museum and get away before any authorities become alerted.

The sense of responsibility hung heavy around his neck. There was more on the line here than just Heung-min's life, too, though that of course was the absolute priority. Large parts of the Tripitaka Koreana was still missing. Jae-won also needed urgent medical attention on his shot-up leg, yet he was now at the mercy of the very person tasked with protecting the museum. If the young guard changed his mind, or the older guard regained his senses at the wrong time, his friend could end up spending a decade behind bars, or worse. That in turn would leave his children without a father and a wife without a husband.

None of that bore thinking about as Kane began his pursuit of the inconspicuous little vase so sought after by Katashi-fucking-Goto.

Kane sprinted the short distance towards the display

case protecting the ancient Japanese artefact known as the Vase of Heaven. When he reached it he took a moment to appraise the modest artefact, working out the best way to remove it from the case without risking damage to the vase itself. After half a dozen seconds, Kane had to admit he didn't see how it was possible. The object sat nestled on its small stand surrounded by a cube of what seemed to be two-inch-thick toughened glass. There appeared to be no visible locking system, and the glass cube sat upon a solid-looking base, seemingly all one structure. It was becoming clear that an act of violence was the only way to access the artefact.

Kane glanced about for some kind of solid instrument, hoping to find a fire hydrant or better still, a fire axe. There was nothing of that kind anywhere in his vicinity. Time was ticking. The longer he took, the greater the risk of being caught. Kane inhaled. He had to attack the display case using himself as the instrument.

He took a couple of steps back from the display and flexed his muscles. This could go so terribly wrong in so many ways, and Kane had a vision of successfully breaking the glass but then the glass severing vital arteries in his legs.

He had no choice but to try, and with another quick inhale, and one final slow exhale, Kane took two determined strides towards the display case and launched himself into a flying two-footed straight-legged kick.

One second later Kane found himself sprawled on the tiles, pain shooting through his right knee. He glanced up; and saw no discernible damage done to the display case.

Well, shit, he thought as he hauled himself up from the floor, sheepishly glancing around as if his failure had been seen.

He exhaled, stepped back and prepared to try again,

although he didn't expect any better result this time either. Again, his feet collided with the glass case with tremendous force, but it was no use. It was impenetrable without some kind of hard object. *Or a gun...*

Kane darted back around the corner and stopped short. The old guard stood there in front of both Nam-gil and Jae-won, his gun raised and trained on them, though his eyes now found Kane.

"Come over here and join us," he said. "Or I will shoot."

Kane held his hands out in a submissive gesture, though he commenced edging slowly forwards, one small step at a time.

Surely the old man won't actually shoot now he's got us under control?

Yet Kane had underestimated people before, with tragic consequences. He would not do it this time. Nor ever again.

"As I explained to young Nam-gil," Kane said gently, "there has been a serious misunderstanding."

"It is true," Nam-gil said in his native Korean, "these are good men who need our help."

"Silence!" demanded the old guard called Jeong-sil.

To Kane, the man had an aura about him that belied his rather meek appearance. Kane couldn't know for sure, but it seemed as if he had an air of authority, perhaps from a military background, and not just the mandatory service Nam-gil was currently on. Kane wondered fleetingly if he was old enough to have even served in the Korean War, though that would put him at about ninety... he was old, but not *that* old.

"Please," Jae-won said from the floor, also in Korean. "It is my son... he has been kidnapped. I have to take an artefact in exchange for his life. You must let us go. Please."

"Why the hell should I believe that? Sounds like a load of bullshit to me."

Kane had edged a further few slow steps towards the group of three men; two captives and one captor. He couldn't just let this fail now because of the duty of one old man, albeit admirable.

Kane watched as the old guard reached for his walkie talkie on his belt. It looked as if he was about to call in reinforcements... or more likely, the police.

Kane could not let that happen.

He *would not* let that happen.

It was now or never. He had to stop the man making the call, even if it meant risking himself or Jae-won taking a bullet.

It was a risk he was more than willing to take and after thinking about it for a full second, he knew Jae-won would be willing to take that same risk.

Kane yelled as loud as he could to startle and distract the old man, and charged, closing the twenty or so feet between them in three seconds.

The old man spun upon hearing Kane's yell, and as he turned and raised the gun at Kane, Nam-gil heroically flung himself at his superior's legs, toppling him off balance and as the guard fired, the shot screamed past Kane's ear and smashed a nearby glass display case, showering shards everywhere.

Kane reached the old man and shouldered him to the ground, then pinned him down as Nam-gil recovered and came to his aid.

"Over there," Nam-gil said, motioning with his head to a discreet door nestled into the gallery wall. "Store room."

Kane nodded. Less than two minutes later, the old guard Jeong-sil was safely locked in the store room, unharmed, and relieved of any communications devices. Kane had taken his gun, and with a nod of thanks to Nam-gil, and a nod of encouragement to Jae-won, Kane once more made his way towards the artefact that was causing them all so much trouble.

As he reached it, he stopped, took the safety off the gun and aimed carefully at the bottom left corner of the thick glass cube. He fired. The first round left a huge dent in the glass. As expected, the piercing high-pitched scream of the security alarm rang out around the entire complex. He didn't have much time. It would still take several more shots. One by one, Kane fired into the cube, until at last, the whole of one side shattered, and left a space big enough for Kane to retrieve the Vase of Heaven.

He grabbed the small vase carefully and slotted it gently into the backpack he'd been wearing, wrapped in a padded blanket. Two minutes later, Kane was flying down the external staff stairs to the ground floor and a minute after that, he had scrambled back over the perimeter fence and was racing along the edge of the river before trudging up into the forest, making his way back towards the ancient bridge, where he slowed his pace, checking for any unwanted company.

Just moments later, he was in Jae-won's car, and was soon easing his way along back roads out of Gyeongju and towards the sprawling metropolis of Daegu, and to who knew what dangers that might await him.

Chapter Thirty-Five

Nam-gil helped Jae-won to his feet.

The alarms continued to ring out around the complex, and were almost painful to Jae-won's ears. They struggled along a few yards, Nam-gil with his arm beneath Jae-won's armpit, and paused to rest at a bench set against a wall.

"In my training," Nam-gil said, "we were told that the police would arrive in a maximum of five minutes if the alarm system was ever triggered. I do not... I am not sure we can make it out of here in time." He didn't say it—it didn't need saying—but he nodded with concern towards Jae-won's injured leg.

Jae-won grunted. While he didn't want to be arrested, the most important thing was that Kane had gotten away with the artefact. In his mind, Jae-won was willing to accept whatever punishment he received for his part in the robbery. Still, he was not going to give up easily, especially since he had total faith that his friend had started the downtown fire as planned, and that the majority of the city's police would have been called to that instead of to the museum.

"I understand. Let's go," Jae-won said, rousing himself to his feet again and ignoring the searing pain that still coursed through his body from his bullet wound. He'd lost a lot of blood, but not enough that he feared for his life.

Perhaps my tae-kwon-do days are over, he mused mirthlessly as they limped along towards the elevators. *A small price to pay for the safety of my son.*

He had considered trying to leave via the climate control room through which they'd arrived. Instead, Jae-won figured that, because of his injury, negotiating the narrow walkway and then three flights of stairs would almost certainly diminish his chances of getting away speedily enough before the police came. Instead, they were going to walk right out through the front doors and take their chances that the police would be delayed long enough to allow their escape.

Now twenty miles outside Gyeongju and safely away from the museum, Kane finally had a moment to settle himself down and think about what might come next.

As he'd left the city via the north, before joining the Gyeong-bu Expressway towards Daegu, he'd seen from across the river the huge blaze arranged by Jae-won and made reality by his friend. It lit up the entire area and was probably visible for many miles in the clear, bitterly cold night sky. As he gazed at the flames reflected in the slow flowing Nam-chon River, Kane only hoped the blaze wouldn't affect anyone's lives too much. He felt confident Jae-won would never deliberately risk anyone's livelihoods, and especially not their lives, and Kane rested easy as he merged onto the highway that would lead him west to Daegu.

He glanced at the digital clock on the dashboard. 10:47 pm. It was thirty-six minutes since the video message from Katashi. That technically gave him a little less than ninety minutes to locate the warehouse the anonymous contact had given them, and first analyse the scene to see if there was any way of rescuing Heung-min without the need to hand over the artefact. Kane knew the distance was only about forty or so miles. So, he had time. But did he have the knowledge? Had that anonymous message been some kind of trick? Was he walking into a death trap?

Kane couldn't help but wonder what his real role in all of this was. He knew Katashi Goto felt he owed Kane, and not in a good way. Kane had been instrumental in the former Yakuza don being caught and arrested after their last meeting, during which Kane had defied the mafia boss in his quest to steal another ancient artefact. Kane had lost a finger in the incident, shot off by one of Katashi's thugs. Kane had got the better of the mobster and his men that fateful night in Japan several years earlier. Would he again? Was this all about Katashi's revenge over Kane? And was the kidnapping of Heung-min all just a ploy to lure Kane to his death?

Kane could not believe the old man would actually be here in Korea in person. He was not only supposed to be dead, but he was also a very old man. When Kane had last seen him he was on death's door and had only survived the helicopter fall by some kind of miracle. And could he even travel? On what passport? In secret?

None of that made any sense to Kane, and he did not expect to lay eyes on Katashi Goto.

Kane had no way of knowing any of these answers, but there was one thing he did know for certain: he was going to get Heung-min safely away from the deranged gangster, or his men, even if it meant sacrificing his own life in the process.

Kane kept his pace steady, despite the required urgency. The last thing he needed was to be pulled over for speeding. It wasn't long until he reached the outskirts of Daegu. He knew the city, but not that well. He had visited before with Jae-won and his family several years earlier on his last trip to Korea. They had come here to climb the city's highest peak, Biseul-san, for the views it afforded over the city and the larger mountains beyond to the west.

That had been a lovely day. Kane knew this night-time visit would be nothing of the sort.

He entered the metropolis from the east and followed the signs to the airport situated in the north of the city, before cutting back south towards the downtown area. The address given by the anonymous source was in west downtown, not too far from the famous Seo-mun Market, which Kane knew to be a bustling industrial area with a lot of warehouses, many of which were derelict and abandoned. Kane understood that it was the perfect place in which to conduct shady business.

His mind then drifted to the Tripitaka. He so desperately wanted to ensure its safe return to the temple complex at Haeinsa. Yet, as important as that was, both to Kane, and more crucially, the Korean nation, it would have to be of a secondary concern until Heung-min was free and safe.

Kane felt a knot form in his guts. It was an all-too familiar feeling, but rather than unsettle and unnerve him, to Kane it served as motivation. It heightened his senses for the challenges to come. It served as something on which to focus his attention, to keep his mind on the job at hand. Fear, for that's what it was essentially, was to be embraced.

Kane knew that all too well.

Chapter Thirty-Six

"Now then, why did you have to corrupt our little Mika?"

The team's Japanese leader spoke Korean fluently, though he didn't like to. To his ears it was an ugly language spoken by ugly, uncultured people.

Kenji's boot collided with the back of Heung-min's skull so hard it even elicited a gasp or two from his colleagues. Their main boss—most of them had never met Katashi Goto and knew of him through reputation only—had made it clear that the man they'd kidnapped was not to be overly harmed, at least not yet. However, their team leader Kenji had really laid into him this time.

Kenji stood over Heung-min's unmoving body, the hint of a grin curling his thin lips. "It is not that I don't enjoy beating up lesser humans. I actually do. It is just that I do not like disobeying the orders of my boss. Yet, you left me no choice. I have a job to do, and you have made that job more difficult. Nevertheless, it will not detract from the success of this mission." Kenji paused and leaned over a little, just to check his victim was still breathing.

Heung-min was breathing, though he was barely conscious.

Kenji inhaled. "It matters little. But by sending that message out via Mika, well, there are always consequences for our actions. Do you know what you have done?" Kenji nudged Heung-min in the back with his foot. Heung-min grunted but remained still. "Well, she has paid for your actions with her life. We simply cannot allow one person to undermine our hierarchy or our collective project."

Heung-min's head shifted just a little, as if he'd registered Kenji's words but wasn't yet able to react.

Kenji continued. "Yes, she had to be punished, at the very least to make an example for the rest of the team. She will be dismantled methodically, piece by piece like a machine, and she will simply disappear, probably in the nearby river. I will undertake that work myself. I suspect that will also be your fate soon enough."

Kenji turned to his men. "Give him some more. A lot more. But do not kill him."

"Hai!" the men responded in unison. *Yes!*

Kenji took his mobile phone from his pocket and switched on the video camera feature and pressed record as three of his team went to work kicking and punching their stricken Korean prisoner with vicious power. He remained still, and anyone who just happened to walk in on the proceedings would surely assume the body was already just that, a body, such was the force of the beating.

"Enough," Kenji finally said and the men obeyed, dragging Heung-min by his arms and hauling his inert form against a wall, propping him up so his face was visible to the camera.

Kenji checked the recording, and after pressing a couple

of buttons, he sent the video to Heung-min's father's mobile phone.

Kane glanced over at the mobile phone on the passenger seat. It was Jae-won's phone, but both agreed it was better for Kane to keep the phone with him since Jae-won was more or less out of the game now anyway.

Checking his mirrors for any unwanted police presence nearby, Kane grabbed up the phone and hit play on the video attached to the text message. His eyes went wide in horror again as he watched Heung-min receiving his terrible beating at the hands of the cowardly men smashing into him with boots and their fists. The barrage lasted a full two minutes and once again Kane wondered, despite how tough he knew Heung-min was, how he could have survived that assault.

He wasn't sure why I watched it again, but supposed it was to sharpen his mind on the task at hand. He wished more than anything it was himself and not Heung-min who was taking that brutal assault, and Kane's eyes narrowed and his jaw set firm. Grinding his teeth, he pressed a little harder on the accelerator as he closed in on what he thought might very well be the scene of his friend's son's murder.

Heung-min heard the three or four sets of boots clomp out of the room and the door get shut and locked behind them. He inhaled slowly, which caused shooting pains in his chest from what he assumed where cracked or broken ribs. He recalled the words the apparent leader had said. Dismantled? Disappear in the river?

The fucking cowards, he thought. Heung-min felt a sudden sense of despair. He had encouraged the girl to help him, and they had killed her for it. *Bastards!*

Exhaling, he did a mental check of his head and body for injuries. There were a lot of painful bruises and several cuts and gashes he couldn't see, but could definitely feel. He tentatively reached a hand behind his head to feel the result of the hardest kick he'd received. There was indeed a huge lump forming, but the skin at least wasn't broken. Nausea roiled in his guts from the pain. And the ribs. That's where most of the pain was focused and he guessed at least two were cracked, if not completely broken. He was indeed in pain, but pain he could handle. Other than that, he wasn't in as bad shape as he thought the assailants believed he was.

Considering the accumulation of multiple injuries, and the intensity of the beating they'd given him, physically, Heung-min was fine. So fine, in fact, that despite it all, he felt himself smiling in the darkness.

Is that all you've got, you cowardly motherfuckers?

And then Heung-min heard himself chuckle.

Chapter Thirty-Seven

Nam-gil's heart was pumping fast as he helped Jae-won hobble out of the elevator and shuffle along towards the museum entrance. The older man's trouser leg was drenched and he was losing a lot of blood, and fast. Both men knew they needed to get out of there quickly, but their passage on foot was painfully slow due to Jae-won's injury.

Just then they both heard the distant yet unmistakable screech of police sirens somewhere to the west coming from the direction of downtown Gyeongju. The detained older guard must have somehow found a way to raise the alarm. From the main central police station it was only a five- or six-minute drive to the National Museum, but thankfully the falling snow had settled and would make the drive more hazardous and slower on the treacherous provincial roads.

"I think maybe ten minutes," Nam-gil told Jae-won.

Jae-won grunted. He thought the same.

The snow now fell heavily, whipping around their faces and bodies on a freezing wind that bit at their skin through their clothes and stung their eyes. Jae-won tried to ignore it as his mind focused on Heung-min, consumed with worry for his kidnapped son. Was he okay? Had Kane successfully found the warehouse?

Is Heung-min still alive?

Jae-won gritted his teeth against both the pain and his fear as they made agonisingly slow progress towards the younger man's car, unfortunately parked in the staff area at the far end of the car park. Jae-won's injury made it difficult to even stay on his feet. Nam-gil was doing his best to support him, but he wasn't a strong man and was clearly struggling to keep his footing too.

Nam-gil had offered to go and get the car and come back to collect Jae-won, but both had agreed that if the police came before Nam-gil returned it would have left Jae-won out in the open and unable to flee.

The police sirens grew louder, and Jae-won knew they were running out of time. He gritted his teeth again and pushed himself harder, his eyes scanning the parking lot for any sign of danger.

Finally, they reached the car. Nam-gil helped Jae-won into the passenger seat. Jae-won winced and groaned in pain as he slumped back into the seat.

Nam-gil hurried around to the driver's side door and scrambled inside, slamming the door shut and fumbling with the keys as he struggled to get them from his pocket.

"Come on," Jae-won growled. Nam-gil mumbled an apology.

Finally he got the key into the ignition and turned. Nothing. He tried again, and still nothing happened.

"Start the damned engine," Jae-won grunted urgently, his eyes finding the rearview mirror but seeing nothing of concern.

Nam-gil exhaled and turned the key again. Silence. "I

am sorry... it is an old car, and in this cold... I am sorry." He turned the key again, and again, the engine remained silent.

Jae-won muttered something Nam-gil couldn't discern and started to open his door. But this time, when Nam-gil tried the key again, the car spluttered for a moment before coughing to life. He turned to Jae-won, a relieved expression brightening his face. Jae-won only nodded.

Through the perimeter fence in front of the car they both saw the iconic red and blue glow of the police cars light the sky as they appeared into view, still perhaps a mile away, across the main road and beyond the grounds of the nearby Anapji temple complex.

"Go, now!" demanded Jae-won. Nam-gil duly obliged.

The car lurched backwards, tires struggling for purchase on the slick, snow-covered tarmac as they edged away from the fence, but when the treads bit, Nam-gil skilfully steered them towards the exit.

The police were closing in, their sirens wailing as they careened towards them along the main highway, faster than Jae-won had expected considering the conditions. He glanced down at his leg. He knew it needed treating. He knew that at the very least he would need the bullet removed and some surgical expertise to repair the damage. He also knew Heung-min was still a captive of that madman Katashi. His friend Hiram had gone there alone. Jae-won could not just sit back and not help his son, nor could he in good conscience not try and help his friend.

"Daegu!"

Nam-gil turned to his ailing passenger. "What? Daegu? No, you must go to a hospital. Your leg... you're still bleeding. I insist—"

"I said take me to Daegu!" Jae-won glared at the young

guard. He had already helped them so much. He was risking his job. His career. Dishonourable discharge from his military duty. He had risked too much already, but Jae-won needed him now and the glare he shot at Nam-gil left the young man in no doubt as to their destination. Nam-gil nodded and headed for the exit gates.

They passed through the gates and turned immediately left, onto the back road that led over the road bridge, then across the river that ran parallel to Wolseong Forest to the south, the route Jae-won and Kane had taken to the museum what seemed like a lifetime ago but was in fact less than an hour.

"Stop here a moment," Jae-won instructed, "and turn off the lights."

Nam-gil did as asked. Both men arched their necks to look through the back window. Just thirty seconds later, a convoy of four police cars, their lights flashing and their sirens screeching into the night sky, raced around the corner into view and then passed through the gates to the Gyeongju National Museum.

Jae-won nodded, then turned to Nam-gil. "Gam-sa hap-ni-da," he said quietly. *Thank you.* "Now take me to Daegu. And drive fast."

Nam-gil drove them along the back roads and out of the small city of Gyeongju, and soon they were on the expressway heading west to Daegu.

As they cruised west as fast as was safely possible along the snow-covered expressway, the huge snowflakes rushing at the windscreen making visibility limited if not quite impossible, Jae-won's mind was consumed with worry for his son. As if on autopilot, he had managed to tie a strip of material from his shirt around his calf above the wound and the bleeding had more or less stopped. It would need treating soon, but he would not die from the injury.

Jae-won knew that, with Nam-gil's help, he would do everything in his power to get to the warehouse and try and help Kane retrieve Heung-min.

And given the chance, he would make Katashi-fucking-Goto wish he'd never been born!

Chapter Thirty-Eight

Kane soon located the address the anonymous source had given them and pulled gently to a stop one street back from the warehouse. He checked the time. 11:28pm. There was still half an hour before Katashi's deadline. Still time to scope the scene and try to extract Heung-min on the quiet.

Kane exited the car and gently slung on the backpack containing the precious artefact. Then, at a trot, he navigated his way along the dimly lit street towards the address. A light snow had persisted and the temperature had dropped significantly since leaving Gyeongju; it was now a little below freezing, Kane suspected. He wasn't dressed for it and hustled a little faster against the chill.

He paused at a dark corner and surveyed the scene. Directly across from him was the warehouse relative to the address. On either side of it stood two large buildings, also warehouses by the looks of them. They appeared abandoned; no lights glowed from within. The central building however did have lights on inside, and Kane crossed the road and ducked into the weak shadows created by the sporadic street lamps that did little to illuminate the area, and instead caused an eerie washed-out orange glow, only accentuated by the lazily falling snow. The scene seemed almost apocalyptic, and Kane had seen enough Korean movies that he half expected a herd of Yong Sang-ho's zombies from the "Train to Busan" movie come ambling around the corner.

Ignoring his over-active imagination, Kane scanned the building for a discreet entry point. There were several external, rusted metal stairways that led to the building's upper levels, though they looked as if they hadn't been used in decades. Kane abstractedly tried to recall when he'd last had a tetanus shot. He did see large industrial doors on the ground floor, next to which was a personnel entrance, but he decided not to attempt to enter via those.

Hey boys, hello, I'm here. Kane almost grinned. Almost. This wasn't funny. He opted for one of the precarious-looking stairways.

Just then a soft ping alerted Kane to an incoming text. He stepped back into the shadows and snagged the phone from his pocket and opened the message. It was another video. He hit play.

On the screen, the video showed a hooded figure being led into a dark room. A single spotlight illuminated the space. Two men, one either side of the figure, escorted him to a chair that sat in the centre of the room and forced him roughly onto the seat. The figure's head lolled to the left, and it appeared to Kane as if he was either barely conscious or heavily drugged. Either way he was putting up little resistance.

Heung-min? Kane had to assume it was.

There was very little noise on the video, until a man, out of shot, said in accented English, "Time is up." Then, also from out of camera view, another man, this one masked, entered the scene and without warning, raised a gun and shot the hooded figure in the head. The body slumped off the chair onto the floor, dead!

"Nooooo!" Kane growled. "Heung-min? No, no, nooooo!"

For long seconds Kane stood there, eyes blinking rapidly, as if he couldn't quite understand what he'd just seen.

A murder? In cold blood?

That's how it seemed. It didn't make any sense. Kane wasn't yet late. There was still time before the deadline set by Katashi. Why would they kill Heung-min now? What was to gain by removing the object with which they were to trade? Something didn't add up. Then again, this was Katashi Goto. A man who had faked his own death. A career criminal, and one-time leader of the most feared Yakuza gang in all Japan. A fucking madman.

The more he thought about it, the less he believed they had actually killed Heung-min. He could think of no obvious reason they would do that, and with a little hope returning that Heung-min was still alive, Kane stowed the phone away and bustled across the road.

Moments later he found himself on a mezzanine platform that circumambulated the exterior of the building, and soon located an old window, its glass half missing. He pulled his sleeve down over his hand and in a few seconds had removed the last fragments of the broken pane. With a grunt, Kane hauled himself up onto the rotting windowsill and peered into the gloomy interior. Immediately inside the threshold, all was still and silent. Across the vast space stood several doors, all closed. Between those doors were nestled a series of windows, some of which revealed shadowy movements beyond.

Bingo!

He shrugged off the backpack containing the Vase of Heaven and stowed it beneath the window. Then, as carefully and quietly as possible, Kane eased himself through the window frame and dropped onto the unkempt floorboards within, cursing as one creaked beneath his weight. He froze, expecting the noise to have alerted those within to his presence, but nothing happened. Sticking to the exterior wall, Kane hustled along the inside, making a circuit of the sprawling warehouse space, treading as lightly as possible as he closed in on the first window. The glass was opaque and reinforced with wire, making it impossible to see through clearly. Kane thought he could make out three figures in that room, two standing, and one seated at a table. He heard soft chatter but couldn't make out any words. It was certainly not Korean, though. It was Japanese. He was close.

Kane shuffled silently along to the next window, ducking down below the sill. This window, with clear glass rather than translucent, revealed only one occupant in the room beyond. The man, dressed in what looked like military style fatigues, all black, sat slumped back in a chair, his head resting on the wall behind him. He was sound asleep. Next to him in the far corner stood a door with a sign that stated it was a store room in Korean. The man had a semi-automatic rifle resting in his lap. Kane's heart beat a little faster.

Putting two and two together, Kane figured the man was probably guarding a prisoner.

Heung-min.

Chapter Thirty-Nine

Heung-min heard the gun shot. He'd drifted off into a half doze and the booming sound rattled in his head, which still ached from the hefty kick he'd received from the leader of whoever these bastards were.

Who the hell have they shot now? Who the fuck are these people?

He gazed around the darkened room they still kept him chained up and locked in. He remained attached to the old-style radiator and although he'd tried everything, he could not get free of the metal bonds around his wrists.

His body ached, not only from the beating he'd taken earlier, but from his many hours—*was it days now?*—he'd been confined in that hard wooden chair, with little or no ability with which to move or stretch his long frame. Yet he was still alive. Judging by what the leader had told him about the girl who'd apparently helped him, and the gun shot he'd just heard, Heung-min knew that for now at least, he was the lucky one.

He wondered if the girl, Mika, had actually managed to get a message out to his family. He worried about them.

They were a tight-knit family, and although Heung-min and his father didn't always see eye to eye, they were close. His mother and his little sister would be beside themselves with worry. He had never once given them cause to worry about his whereabouts and would always check in with them at least once every day whilst he was away at university. He felt guilty for putting them through this, though of course he was blameless. Still, he felt distraught that he'd let himself be so easily taken by these... *what even are they? Gangsters? Terrorists?*

He still had no idea who they were. He had ascertained for certain that the leader was Japanese, as were most of the thugs he'd encountered during the beatings. They had never revealed who they were or who they worked for, nor had they ever mentioned what their goals were. He had overheard the word Tripitaka a few times. Heung-min, like all Koreans, knew all about the Tripitaka Koreana, the revered collection of carved wooden tablets that formed the world's largest, most complete collection of carved Buddhist texts. Although Heung-min had studied a little Japanese, he hadn't been able to make out any other words.

Have they stolen it? Surely that's impossible? And what the hell has that got to do with me?

Right now, Heung-min wasn't sure who these people were, or what they wanted with him. Nor had he any idea what their endgame was. However, he was certain it wasn't good, and that it likely wouldn't end well for him personally.

One thing he knew for sure, though, was that if his father had received a message from the girl, and had been informed where he was being held, there was no doubting he would be pulling out all the stops to get his son back to his family, whatever that took. His father was a brave, proud man, who would never allow anything to happen to his beloved family. He knew his father to be an upstanding, well-respected member of the local community, as he had always been wherever they had lived. He had never broken a law in his life, Heung-min was certain of that.

Yet he had always wondered what his father was really capable of. Physically, there were few men to match him on the tae-kwon-do mat and Heung-min believed that deep down, his father was capable of great violence, though he had never once seen him lose his temper. He was a master of not only the martial art, but of his own discipline. Heung-min had always admired him for it and strived to be more like his father in that, and almost every other respect.

Heung-min hadn't forgotten that his father's close friend Hiram Kane was also on the scene, and that he was somehow involved, albeit probably by accident. He knew enough about Kane and his history to know that he'd been involved in many dangerous international events over the years, and yet had somehow, against the odds, come through them all relatively unscathed.

Is he helping father?

Heung-min couldn't be sure if the girl had even gotten the message out, or if she was just part of the ruse, and he'd been lied to about her murder. None of it was certain, and as he sat there in that cold, airless room, almost in total darkness except for the sliver of light that seeped in beneath the locked door, all Heung-min could do was to remain alert and wait for his opportunity. His tae-kwon-do training had taught him many disciplines, one of which was patience.

And patient he would remain. For Heung-min knew that as soon as the moment arose that would present an opportunity for escape, and perhaps not only escape, but justice, he would be ready to take it.

He closed his eyes and nestled back the best he could

against the radiator. He inhaled deeply through his nose, and let it out slowly through pursed lips. He regulated his breathing, counting ten seconds for each long inhale, held it for a few more, and counted another ten as the air was expelled. He flexed his wrists and knuckles, twisting his neck muscles left and right, up and down, staying as limber as he could.

Just give me one chance, he projected into the darkness. *Just one. I am ready!*

Chapter Forty

Katashi Goto inhaled. He drew his lean, frail shoulders up a little and then relaxed them, letting his hands rest in his lap. He then reached for a cup of tea from a small side table and sipped contentedly as his eyes remained fixed on the large screen mounted on the wall in front of him.

Subconsciously he nodded. On the screen was Hiram Kane, making his way along the interior wall of the warehouse.

"Perfect," he muttered.

Katashi Goto had flown in from Japan via helicopter the night before, using his contacts to avoid any immigration issues at the provincial heliport just outside Daegu's city limits. He hadn't expected any trouble, but when you were officially a dead man, as well as being a criminal wanted for, among other things, murder, extortion, and kidnapping when you were alive, you could never be too careful. Yet humans were weak, Katashi knew, and the lure of money was always a great motivator. His arrival was without incident.

As he watched Kane traverse the warehouse, Katashi considered his plans.

Why am I really here? Are all the risks I've taken worth it?

The answers to those questions were easy. He was here in Korea, a land he once swore he would never set foot in, for one reason only. Revenge. The fact he was set to acquire an artefact worth millions of dollars was a very nice bonus, and the additional fact that he would be delivering a cultural hammer blow to the soul of the Korean people was also a great side dish to his main meal of revenge.

So revenge was the driving force behind this entire endeavour, and the focus of that revenge was currently on the large screen before him.

"Hiram Kane," he whispered, though it was more of a breathy wheeze, "soon we will meet again."

On the screen, Kane had paused at the window to a room in which Katashi knew Kenji was keeping the kid prisoner. He had to admit that it was Kenji's clever idea to involve Kane's friend. Kidnapping the boy was just a little insurance to ensure Kane became involved. So far it was working out well.

Katashi was aware that his reasons for revenge were perhaps not that obvious to anyone who didn't know the full story. Yet to Katashi they were more than justified. Hiram Kane had, quite simply, caused Katashi the most devastating moments of his life. Katashi had been shamed. He had been embarrassed. He had lost face in front of his own men. And ultimately, he had been exposed for what he truly was.

Katashi Goto was a fraud, and in Japanese culture, a fraud of the highest magnitude.

He had claimed samurai heritage for many decades. He had used that heritage to climb the ranks of the Yakuza during the seventies and eighties to its very summit. From humble beginnings as an errand boy, working for low-level gangsters in his own city of Kyoto, he had slowly and steadily scaled the hierarchy of Kyoto's gangland, and while still relatively young in that sordid, deadly underworld, he had become the don of the Kyoto chapter of the Yakuza, the biggest criminal organisation outside of the capital, Tokyo.

What Kane had done was to foil Katashi's plot to steal the infamous samurai suit of armour from the Itsukushima Shrine on Miyajima Island. With that failure, and Katashi's subsequent arrest, it had become known that Katashi was in fact *not* descended from a great lineage of samurai warriors, and was instead nothing more than the son of a peasant farmer, who in turn was from a long line of peasant farmers.

The embarrassment of this bombshell was something Katashi knew he would never overcome, and from the moment he had conceived of the idea to fake his own death and thus escape from prison, he had only one last thing left to achieve in life before his real death, which was not too far in the future... if his doctor could be trusted.

A couple of years earlier he had scoffed when the ridiculously well paid, and professionally corrupt doctor, had told him he had months to live. The cancer was more advanced than the doctor had first thought, and he had solemnly informed Katashi that he should make plans for his estate after his death.

Now Katashi believed the doctor was right after all. He sensed it, as well as felt it. He would soon die, of that he was certain. And as time was running out on Hiram Kane's existence, so too was it running out for Katashi himself.

It matters not, he mused as he took another sip of tea, not caring that it was stone cold. *In less than an hour I will have my revenge.*

Chapter Forty-One

Kane turned away from the window and wedged himself against the wall to the side, out of view in case the armed guard inside woke up. He held still as he scanned the interior of the vast space, and noticed a few small, barely visible CCTV cameras affixed in various spots above.

Katashi, are you watching?

Again, he didn't really believe the old man was actually there in the building. Still, with people like Katashi Goto, you just never knew. Their egos, that ingrained mentality that led them to the top of organisations like the Yakuza, also made them unpredictable and enabled them to make choices that most people would think of as insane. Kane knew all too well, often to his detriment in recent times, it also made them dangerous. He glanced at his hand, the one with the missing finger, shot off by Katashi's men several years earlier.

Where are you, old man?

Kane almost hoped the crazed old bastard was actually there. He inhaled, picturing the former mafia boss, and how he looked these days. On the phone he sounded weak and old, almost certainly sick, based on his wheezy breathing and croaky laugh. Kane believed he must also be well into his eighties by now. Not a physical threat, but the man did exude an aura, and there was no doubt he was, or had at least once been, a feared leader of men.

Kane didn't know if Katashi was there or not, but anyone who was there working for him would certainly be formidable adversaries.

Kane readied himself. He had no plan other than to attempt to overpower the dozing guard and get to Heung-min before anyone else could notice. He would then try to use the vase to bargain their way out of there. It wasn't a great plan, but now he was alone, after Jae-won's injury, it was the best he could come up with.

He edged along the wall and paused at the window, then poked his head around to look inside and found himself face to face with the business end of a semi-automatic rifle. The guard holding it sneered.

"Do not move!" came an authoritative voice from behind him.

Kane turned to see several figures walking with intent in his direction. They were all clad in black fatigues, and though Kane didn't immediately notice any weapons, he had to assume they each had one or more concealed about their person.

The four figures, three men and a woman, approached out of the shadows from different directions, closing in on Kane in a semi-circle formation.

He was trapped.

"Hiram Kane. So nice of you to join us." One of the men addressed Kane, his accented English precise but devoid of any hint of emotion. The man who had spoken stepped a little closer as the other three closed ranks beside him.

Kane appraised the group. The men were tall, and certainly athletic, and looked as if they knew their way around a gym. The woman was less formidable physically but she had moved with grace, and Kane suspected she too was more than capable in a fight. All three of them had fixed their gazes on Kane, though their expressions remained blank, focused... dangerous.

Kane's eyes drifted to the central man who had spoken to him, their apparent leader. This guy was not as tall as the other two men, but his shoulders were broad and Kane recognised in his eyes a look he had seen too often in recent years. To someone less experienced in these types of situations—Kane wished he wasn't as well versed—those eyes betrayed little. No emotion. No sense of purpose. No nothing. And that was what concerned Kane. He felt sure he was looking into the eyes of a killer.

"Who are you?" Kane asked. "Let me guess, you're Katashi's puppets? What, is the old man too afraid to face me himself?"

The leader's head tilted a little to the side, as if weighing up Kane. Kane watched as the man inhaled slowly, as if this was all just a little boring.

"It matters not, but my name is Kenji. Do you have the artefact?" he asked in a monotone.

Kane said, "Is the kid still alive?"

The leader's eyes narrowed slightly. He glanced over Kane's shoulder to the guard inside the room. He gave a slight nod. Kane turned and saw the guard go to the door in the corner and knock. A moment later, the door swung open and another man also dressed in the same black fatigues led a hooded figure into the centre of the room. The first guard then yanked off the hood.

Kane gasped. There stood Heung-min. His face was bruised and swollen, and blood had dried on several cuts and gashes. One eye was almost closed because of swelling. He was too far away to get a sense of Heung-min's mental state or if he was even coherent. Kane could see enough to know the poor kid had suffered some terrible physical abuse.

"Let him go!" Kane had turned back to the leader. "Let him go now!"

The man named Kenji smirked. "Or what? It does not seem to me that you are in a position to make demands."

Kane expelled air through gritted teeth. He stepped forward, a move that was matched by the three surrounding guards. Kane still didn't see any weapons.

"You must be such a brave man to have first kidnapped and then assaulted a kid." Kane edged forward another couple of feet. He narrowed his eyes. "Why don't you try your luck with me?"

For the first time, Kenji's eyes crinkled just the slightest bit in amusement. His lip curved almost imperceptibly into a smile. Kane sensed the man was itching to fight him.

Instead, Kenji spoke calmly. "My boss would like to speak with you."

"Is he here? Is Katashi here in this building?"

Now Kenji smiled. "Of course he is not. He is dead."

Chapter Forty-Two

"But you knew that already," the leader said.

For just a brief moment, Kane wondered if Katashi really was dead, and that he'd been conned into believing he was still live. That doubt lasted only seconds.

"He has been dead for years now. Nevertheless, he still wants to speak with you."

Kane inhaled. *So the old bastard is here. Well, then, so be it.*

"Okay," Kane said with some reluctance—he didn't know how he'd react to seeing the man responsible for this latest disaster, and didn't trust himself not to lose his mind with rage. "Lead the way."

The lead man, Kenji, nodded and turned. Kane made to follow, then without warning he took two powerful strides forward and launched himself off his right leg, leading with his left, then brought his right leg around again so hard that when it connected with the leader's temple it dropped him to his knees. Kane landed perfectly on two feet and crouched into a fighting stance, ready for the assault he felt sure would come from the other three aggressors.

Yet they didn't attack as he'd expected. Kenji recovered in an instant and rose to his feet, spinning to face Kane. He focused on Kane's eyes, amusement resonating in his own.

One of the guards muttered something to his leader that Kane didn't catch. Kenji shook his head and the guard backed away a couple of steps.

Kane felt his heartbeat ratchet up a notch.

So he does want to fight. Good!

Kane and Kenji watched each other warily, appraising the other's movements, two hard men ready to take the fight to the other. Their eyes locked. Kane could feel the tension building inside him as he waited for Kenji to make a move. They circled slowly, each taking short, deliberate steps to the left.

All around them, silence reigned. Kane could hear nothing other than his pulse pounding in his ears and an icy draft whistling through a broken window somewhere high above. He glanced at the other three guards, spectators to the fight about to happen. They watched him passively, indifferent to him, as if his outcome was already determined and they were just waiting for the inevitable.

Kane focused back on Kenji. He had administered a thunderous kick to the man's head but he had recovered almost instantly; clearly he was a hard man and not to be taken lightly. Kane considered his next move. He obviously couldn't win a fight against all four of these guards, most likely all skilled fighters and almost certainly armed. One at a time? Kane fancied his chances against any individual adversary in a fair fight. But there were four of them and they would not fight fair, of that he was certain. He needed a different plan, one that didn't involve risking his life unnecessarily.

Then, inexplicably, Kenji said, "Enough! Where is the artefact?"

They don't know?

Kane felt sure they had somehow been watching his approach. This knowledge gave him time, if nothing else.

"Let the kid go."

"It doesn't matter if you tell us where it is. We know you have successfully removed it from the museum. Our man there has already told us."

Kane realised Kenji must have been referring to the old guard. Or was he? Did he actually mean Nam-gil? If so, that meant Jae-won was in serious trouble. He didn't respond yet.

"We know you left the museum with it and that it is here somewhere. I have people searching for it right now. But if you tell me where it is, it will save us all some time." He flicked his head towards the room in which Heung-min was being held. "And it might even save some serious pain... So tell me, Mr Kane, where is the vase?"

"I do not trust you," Kane stated. "Once you have the vase, how do I know you will let the kid go?"

Kenji grinned, though it didn't reach his dark eyes. "You don't."

Suddenly, Kenji lunged forward and struck Kane's chin with such force that it stunned him onto one knee. Down, but more out of shock than actual injury. Kane's gaze rose to meet Kenji's and he rose too, standing tall and not showing any effects from the solid blow. Kane nodded.

Fair enough, he thought, not feeling as if the surprise attack was a cowardly move, *I did smash you when your back was turned.*

"Listen to me, Mister Kane. Our boss, who you know as

Katashi Goto, has no interest in killing the boy. He has merely used him to get you involved. The reasons for that are not my concern. I have my orders, and I will execute those orders to the letter."

"What about the Tripitaka?" Kane asked. "Was it you who stole it and damaged the temple?"

Kenji nodded. "I am told what to do by my boss, and I do it, without question. Yes, that was me and my team. Again, Katashi cares little for that... that dusty old pile of relics. That was also just a part of his bigger plan. And here you are."

Kane's eyebrows knitted in a frown. "Are you saying Katashi has gone to all that trouble of stealing the Tripitaka, and kidnapping and beating up a kid, not to mention having me steal an ancient vase... all to get me to come to this abandoned... what is it, a warehouse? That is insane... it is the single most ridiculous thing I've ever heard."

Kane really couldn't believe what he was hearing. Surely that was just a load of horse shit. Katashi was many things, maybe even insane, but he was also a smart man. There were many easier ways to have convinced Kane to meet him somewhere. He did not have to involve Jae-won's son. Nor did he have to send men to Jae-won's home at the temple complex and terrify his wife and daughter. He certainly didn't have to damage such an important facet of Korea's cultural heritage. And he did not have to have Kane risk his freedom and maybe even his life to steal a small ancient vase that he didn't even want.

None of it made any sense to Kane, and as he stared at Kenji, the Japanese thug simply shrugged, as if to say, *I know, right? But I do not care!*

Just then another black-clad man entered the arena

from a door in the far corner. Kane's heart sank when he saw the man was holding his backpack, inside of which was the Vase of Heaven. His last bargaining chip was now in the hands of the enemy.

Chapter Forty-Three

Kane knew now that he had nothing left with which to attempt any kind of deal. He doubted these people were the bargaining kind anyway, but that option was now off the table regardless. Kane also suspected that they had never planned to allow him to leave the warehouse alive. If it was all about Katashi's revenge, as it now seemed, then it was only a matter of time until they would overcome Kane and restrain him so Katashi could deal out whatever sick method of revenge the old mob boss had in mind.

Yet Kane still had a job to do. He had to get Heung-min out of there. The Tripitaka was also important to him, but right now there was a young, innocent life on the line and Kane was not about to let these bastards get away with the kidnapping and the cowardly abuse of a friend's son.

It meant only one thing. Kane's eyes drifted to Heung-min. The young man seemed to have collected himself a little since he'd been brought out to the room. He stood to his full height—a solid six foot—and his broad chest seemed puffed out. Despite the external evidence of a beating on his face, Kane thought he looked in reasonable shape. If there were other injuries, Kane couldn't see them. Kane knew Heung-min had followed his father into a life of taekwon-do training. Kane had even sparred with him a little when he was younger, but not for several years, yet he had no doubt he was a formidable proponent of the art. *He must be... he's Jae-won's son.*

Is he ready to fight now? Kane mused.

"Let me speak with the boy. Please," Kane asked Kenji. "I just want to know he's okay."

Kenji nodded and motioned for the guards in the room to bring their captive out into the main warehouse. The two men shoved Heung-min forwards and through the door into the cavernous space. Heung-min's eyes found Kane's and didn't leave them as he was led to stand before him.

"Hello Hiram. It is good to see you," Heung-min said in flawless English, the hint of a grin creeping onto his swollen lips.

"Shit, kid, how are you doing?" Kane said through gritted teeth as he shook his head. Close up the facial injuries appeared worse than he'd thought. He desired to lash out at the cowardly bastards right then but he sensed that was what they wanted. Instead, he fought to remain calm and await the right moment to act. Kane studied Heung-min, appraising him both mentally and physically.

Heung-min seemed to sense Kane's thoughts and said, "I am fine. Just bruises really. In fact, I am ready to party." Heung-min's one open eye closed, and opened again quickly. To Kane it seemed as if it was a wink. Deliberate. *A signal?*

Kane nodded. Heung-min was indeed ready and willing to fight. *Good man,* he thought. Kane saw Heung-min's hands were free. That was a mistake on the part of the captors.

Kane and Heung-min shared a knowing glance. Kane noticed Heung-min inhaling deeply through his nose, preparing himself to act. Kane turned to face Kenji, appraising his position and the positions of the other guards. He was just working out whom he should attack first when Katashi Goto decided to rise from the dead and let Kane know he was alive. The old man entered the warehouse. Although clearly not at all well, Kane now knew he was there to conduct and then witness his imminent death.

Before Kane had time to react, Kenji barked an order and the guards swarmed him. Within seconds both Kane and Heung-min were restrained and forced onto two chairs the guards had positioned in front of the approaching Katashi Goto.

Devastation was what Kane felt in that moment. He felt it in the pit of his stomach. In the way his mouth felt suddenly dry. In the way he had to fight back the tears that threatened to spill. In that instant he knew it was all over. He had failed Heung-min. He had failed his close friend Jae-won. He had failed the Korean people too because Kane knew there was no way these bastards would ever return the Vase of Heaven and they would surely destroy the Tripitaka Koreana.

Kane had also failed himself. As Katashi had stepped into view Kane had let his focus slip. He had allowed his concentration to drift from the task at hand. How had he been so flippant? Had his ego and over-confidence betrayed him? Kane felt the rage burn in his guts. Yet the rage was not for Katashi Goto. It was for himself.

Kane tried hard not to look at Katashi as he stood there before him. He didn't want to give the old Yakuza boss the satisfaction of seeing the defeat written on his face. Yet try as he might, Kane couldn't help but look up at him. He had suspected the old man wasn't really there. He had believed he was too sick to travel, that he was conducting this act from afar, a master of puppets who had these thugs do his bidding from his mansion in Kyoto.

He had been wrong about Katashi's whereabouts. Yet Kane was not wrong about Katashi's health.

The old man was in his eighties, but Kane thought he looked much older than that. When they had last seen each other, despite Katashi's advanced age, he was still in good health and great shape physically. Lean and wiry, he had been tough enough to have survived a hundred-foot fall into shallow water from a helicopter. Now, however, he was stooped over. His shoulders had withered to the size of a young boy's. The skin on his hands and face was leathery and sallow. His once bright eyes were sunken deep into his skull.

Kane thought he looked like a living skeleton.

Katashi stepped closer to Kane, moving in short, shuffling steps with the help of a walking stick. Kane felt two hands push down on his shoulders from behind, as a guard ensured he couldn't attempt to leap from his chair. Another had done the same with Heung-min.

Katashi straightened a little as he stopped in front of Kane. He gazed at Kane with moist eyes, and Kane saw they were bloodshot. Kane spoke first.

"I thought you were dead. I am sorry I was wrong. You do look dead though."

Katashi didn't answer. He gazed at Kane with an expression Kane couldn't fathom. There was no anger in those eyes. No apparent rage. No obvious signal of what the old mob boss was thinking or planning. Kane thought that even if Katashi wanted to strike him, he would barely have the energy. Now he was not worried about what Katashi might do to him or Heung-min physically. Yet he knew the man was cruel. He knew he was capable of terrible acts of violence. These thugs with him would carry out anything he asked of them with cold efficiency and without question.

Katashi smiled. "It is true," he said, "I have seen better days, at least physically." Katashi's words were slow and measured, and uttered in a breathy whisper. "But you should know that my mind is as clear as it has ever been. In fact, my thoughts are more lucid than ever."

That was what worried Kane. In his prime Katashi had been lord of all he purveyed. The very pinnacle of the mafia world in his city and almost all of Japan. What he wanted, he would get.

And apparently, what he wanted was revenge over Kane.

Chapter Forty-Four

"Bring out the winch," Katashi instructed Kenji, who relayed the message to his team. Two of the men trotted off to the far end of the warehouse and opened a set of double doors.

Kane hadn't understood the Japanese words, and turned to look at Heung-min, whom he knew had studied Japanese in school. The younger man looked stoically back at Kane, and sensed the questioning look in Kane's eyes, but he shrugged. He didn't know what they'd said either.

Kane and Katashi gazed down the large warehouse as the two men trundled out a piece of machinery that stood on a pallet. They wheeled the machine on a pallet truck towards the gathering, and Kane's eyes widened as he saw what the object was: a hydraulic winch. He turned to Katashi, who seemed to enjoy the look of horror on Kane's face.

The warehouse was silent, other than the high-pitched squeaking of the rubber wheels of the pallet truck as the men pulled it over the concrete floor. It was an ominous sound, and seemed to Kane to be a portent of the danger to come. A harbinger of pain and suffering.

Katashi didn't say anything. The look in his dark, sunken eyes was enough. He meant to torture Kane, that was obvious now. Kane didn't care what they did to him. His immediate concern was Heung-min.

"This has nothing to do with the kid," he told Katashi. "Whatever issues you have with me are between you and me alone, not this boy. Let him go."

Katashi hobbled over to stand closer to Kane, his walking stick clacking against the cold concrete floor and drawing to Kane's mind the sounds a giant insect might make. "You are right, Hiram," he said passively. "This has nothing to do with the boy. And yet it also has everything to do with him. I know you are a strong man. Resilient. I witnessed that with my own eyes. You can handle pain. This I know. Which is why I am going to make you watch as I have a little fun with your friend."

Kane launched his shoulders up hard and forced his way out from beneath the thug's strong hands and threw himself towards Katashi. But Kenji was poised and ready, and barrelled into Kane with such force that Kane hit the ground hard, his head colliding with the unforgiving concrete and opening a deep gash on his forehead. Two of the other guards closed in and hovered over him, guns drawn and pointed at his head.

"Put him in the chair," Katashi said calmly and the two thugs stowed their weapons and hauled Kane up by his armpits and shoved him back into the chair, this time with his hands secured to it with cable ties.

Blood dripped from the wound into Kane's eyes, but he was powerless to stop it as his hands were bound behind him. He tasted the blood as it dribbled into his mouth and he spat it on the floor. He turned to Heung-min, who looked at him in shock, fear evident in his wide eyes.

"It will be okay," Kane lied, knowing it would be anything but okay. He had to keep the kid on-side and focused. "Nothing will happen to you. Your father will have alerted the police and they will be here soon."

Heung-min nodded. Kane saw his Adam's apple twitch as he swallowed down his fear. Kane knew the lad was tough, but the threat of torture would make anyone fearful.

Bastards. Kane wanted to scream in rage, but he knew that would only entertain Katashi. He tried a different approach.

"Katashi, I beg of you, man to man, let the boy go. He is innocent. He has his whole life in front of him. Do what you want to me. I don't care. Fuck it, I probably even deserve it from you," he lied again, trying in vain to appeal to the old man's ego. "I am... I am sorry for what happened all those years ago."

Katashi surprised everyone then by belying his age and his illness and swiping his walking stick at Kane's head, crashing it viciously into his nose, which exploded in an agonising eruption of blood. Kane slumped to the side, blood pouring from his broken nose. The intense pain caused him to puke, which mixed with the blood on the ground.

Katashi stepped back and glared at Kane, some of the old fire returning to his eyes. "Do not dare apologise to me. You know nothing of what you have done to me and my honour back in Japan. There is nothing you could ever say that could exonerate you from your choices. I have waited a long time for this moment. I am not going to waste it." He turned to Kenji, his dark, grey eyes forming narrow slits of hatred. "String up the boy!"

Chapter Forty-Five

Jae-won gazed through the window as the snow continued to fall in thick, swirling flurries. It wasn't affecting their passage west on the main highway, which remained busy with traffic despite the late hour. Yet beyond the road, deep drifts had started to form on the verges and in the fields, and the snow showed no signs of letting up.

"We will arrive at the outskirts in about ten minutes," Nam-gil told him. "Another ten to reach the downtown area."

Jae-won nodded but didn't answer. His mind was doing its best to conjure up horrific scenarios of what his son might be enduring at the hands of the madman who held him captive. Jae-won had heard Kane mention Katashi Goto in the past and had been horrified of Kane's retelling of the events that had transpired on Miyajima Island, during which several people died and Kane had lost a finger. There had even been a brutal beheading, if Jae-won recalled correctly.

His throat went dry and an icy knot of fear tightened in

his guts as he thought of Heung-min and what his current predicament might be. Despite Jae-won and his family living at and running a temple stay program back in Golgulsa, Jae-won himself wasn't an especially religious man. The temple was Buddhist, and while Jae-won did consider himself Buddhist, he didn't adhere all that strictly to the Buddha's teachings.

Yet despite his tenuous religious beliefs, Jae-won found himself offering up a silent prayer to any god that might be listening to his plea. He asked for his son to be released without any harm befalling him. He asked that his son be returned safe and well and to have not suffered any lasting physical or mental effects from his captivity. He asked for Kane to receive any help he'd need to do what needed to be done.

Finally, he asked for the opportunity to come face to face with his son's captor and his abductor. He wanted a moment to show them both what he thought of their cowardly actions. There would be no need for words. There would be no need for a discussion. There would simply be one man showing other men what happened when you chose the wrong father to mess with.

The last twenty minutes of their drive to downtown Daegu passed in a blur. Jae-won's pain had eased after downing a load of painkillers, and the blood had stopped flowing from the wound. He had managed to clean it with a cloth and some iodine they'd snagged from a late-night pharmacy and wrapped it tightly in a clean bandage they'd also procured. In fact, Jae-won felt pretty good physically as Nam-gil pulled the car to a stop one block away from the address given to them by the anonymous source.

Jae-won still remained a little unsure of the legitimacy of that message, as he now had no way of receiving information from anyone, including Kane. He could only hope that meant the address was indeed legit and that Kane had made his way inside.

"You should stay here," Jae-won stated to Nam-gil. "I appreciate what you have done for me so far. Thank you, but you must stay here in the car."

Nam-gil nodded. Jae-won saw in his eyes that he was considering protesting, but he seemed to have quickly decided against it. Jae-won was aware the young man had already risked his job and his military service. He hoped that once everything was over, the authorities would decide that what he had done was a good thing, and that it wouldn't affect his future.

"I hope you get what you are looking for," Nam-gil replied. "I will... I should get away from here. Is that okay?"

Jae-won nodded and then offered Nam-gil his hand. They shook, and after a quick glance around to check the car was not being watched, Jae-won eased himself quietly out of the vehicle. He shrugged into his jacket in a vain attempt to keep out the bitter cold, and a moment later he made his way towards the warehouse where his son was allegedly being held. His gait was a little awkward due to the injury and the bandages, but the pain was tolerable and he made short work of the two-hundred-yard journey to the building.

Jae-won didn't think he had the time to try and enter stealthily. Nor did he have the patience. He strode to the first door he saw and was surprised to find it unlocked.

Unarmed and unafraid, Jae-won stepped inside and found himself face-to-face with a gun.

Chapter Forty-Six

Two men grabbed Heung-min by his arms and marched him towards the winch. The pallet truck had been removed and the pallet holding the hydraulic winch now sat firmly on the concrete floor of the warehouse.

Heung-min deliberately didn't struggle too much. He wanted to make them believe he was weak and that he posed no threat, and so he let himself easily be shoved towards the contraption. However, he didn't want to make it too easy, and he also wanted to delay the inevitable for as long as possible. Not because he was afraid. In fact, Heung-min felt pretty calm considering the circumstances. He wasn't scared of these men or what they might have planned for him.

He had admired the way Kane had acted, how he had shown no fear or pain when he'd been struck by the old man's stick. It had given him a boost of fortitude that had started to wane when he'd first seen the winch. No, he wanted to delay whatever was about to happen because somehow, he felt certain that salvation was at hand. Somehow, either Kane, or his father, possessed the ability to turn this situation around.

He understood his predicament didn't look good. His father was nowhere close, as far as he knew. Kane was detained and unarmed. They were significantly outnumbered by seemingly ruthless thugs, all armed, and led by a crazed old man who had threatened their lives and who seemed to be someone who didn't make idle threats. No, it did not look good at all.

Yet, for reasons he couldn't quite understand, Heung-min felt sure things would be okay. He cast a sideways glance at Kane, who nodded subtly back at him, his face resolute, as if to say, *Hang in there, kid. The cavalry is coming.*

Whether the cavalry, or the police, or even his father were indeed coming, Heung-min resolved to stay stoic and do whatever he could to get through the unfolding drama.

Suddenly, he let his knees buckle beneath him, and he stumbled to the ground. Both the guards momentarily lost their grip on his arms. He lay there motionless, as if unconscious.

"Can't you see he is sick?" he heard Kane yell out. "Leave him alone for God's sake!" Kane shouted, now struggling against his cable ties, to no avail. Kane seemed to sense Heung-min was faking it and played along. "Just let him go. Please."

The two men hauled Heung-min to his feet, no mean feat considering his size. One of them unleashed a vicious punch to his stomach, just below the two cracked ribs, and this seemed to genuinely hurt Heung-min, making him double over. The guards forced him upright again and shoved him the last few yards to the winch. There they stood, waiting as Katashi slowly walked over to them.

Katashi then picked up a small leather case that had been on the pallet and opened it, perusing the contents within for several seconds before nodding in satisfaction and selecting an item from inside. He turned to Kane, whose eyes had followed his path over towards Heung-min. With a cruel grin, Katashi showed Kane the item he'd selected from the case, and his grin widened further as Kane's eyes did the same.

In his hand Katashi held a cutthroat razor, its steel glinting menacingly beneath the overhead lights.

Jae-won had lost none of his martial arts instincts, and despite his injured leg, the moment he saw the gun he ducked and unleashed a ferocious right tiger claw punch into the man's throat. Jae-won thought he heard the crunch of bone. The guard staggered backwards into a wall and his head collided with the brick with a sickening thud. That did for him, and as he fell unconscious to the ground the weapon clattered to the floor beside him.

Jae-won grabbed it up—some kind of rifle, though Jae-won was not familiar with guns at all—and then quickly closed the door behind him, locking it with a clunk. Turning on his heels, he braced himself to face more guards, but thankfully, none came. He ducked through what was a darkened reception area, with shredded, stained carpets and foisty mould creeping up the walls. A single bulb hung from the ceiling and flickered dimly, causing Jae-won's shadow to dance wildly across the floor.

He approached the next set of doors. Their glass panels afforded him a view into the next room. This was a small yet high-ceilinged store room, which he guessed was an ante-chamber before the main warehouse section of the building. He stayed tight against the wall, trying to be as quiet and subtle as possible. He noticed a CCTV camera mounted on a wall in one corner, its tiny red dot suggesting it was switched on. Grabbing a chair, Jae-won reached up and slung a piece of cloth he'd spotted on the floor over the lens.

It's probably too late, he mused, but did it anyway.

He paused near the doors to listen, but heard nothing other than the wind whistling in beneath a door somewhere, and the gentle cooing of some roosting doves high up in the rafters. No hint of more men, at least not yet. Jae-won quietly swung open one of the glass doors and stepped through into the next room, treading lightly on the concrete floor as he made his way to the far side. Then he spotted another door, slightly ajar, and heard what he thought was muted snoring rumbling from within.

He tiptoed towards the door and peered through the crack between door and frame. Slouched back on an office chair, both feet on the desk in front of him, was a lone guard. On the desk was a huge flat-screen monitor, upon which was displayed a series of views from what Jae-won surmised were various locations around the warehouse.

You just can't get the staff these days, Jae-won thought, as he leaned the weapon against the wall, then hustled over to the guard. Before the guard was even aware of Jae-won's presence Jae-won had gripped him in a crushing neck hold and choked the huge guy until his eyes rolled back in his head and he fell still. Sliding him to the ground, Jae-won pulled the stricken guard into a corner. Then, using a reel of heavy duty packing tape he spotted on a shelf, Jae-won bound the man's hands and feet, and covered his mouth, then strapped him to a hefty steel shelving unit.

With a final check to make sure the man was breathing,

he turned his attention back to the large monitor. He scanned the various screens, which mostly showed dark, empty views of the warehouse. Nothing of interest.

Until he saw something that made his heart miss several beats.

Chapter Forty-Seven

Kane had no doubt Katashi was not making idle threats. He had seen what the sick bastard was capable of, and an image of the old man beheading one of his minions with an ancient samurai sword flashed in his mind. That was the single worst thing Kane had ever witnessed, and he knew he would never forget the horrors of that day.

And yet here he was again, once more at the mercy of the Japanese former crime lord. He suddenly felt helpless, as if he had lost all control over the unfolding situation. He seethed, and pulled against the restraints binding his wrists to the chair beneath him. They didn't give an inch, and he knew trying further was futile.

Kane glanced around the warehouse, searching for anything that might give him hope of escape. There were now six guards—four large men, the fierce looking woman and their apparent leader, Kenji—there with Katashi. Even if he could get loose from his bonds, Kane knew there was no way he could overcome such insurmountable odds.

Perhaps if Heung-min could get free, there might be a slim chance. But Heung-min was not free, and would not be free anytime soon.

Kane watched as Katashi walked slowly past Heung-min, then back again, as if trying to strike fear into the young man. To his credit, Heung-min merely watched him too, never taking his eyes off the old man, as if, Kane thought, to say, *Fuck you, old timer, I am not afraid.*

Kane admired the way the boy was holding it altogether, though he was not at all surprised. His father Jae-won was one of the most humble, disciplined and respectful men he'd ever known. Yet he also had pride and dignity, and Kane was certain that if Jae-won were in the same position as his son now was, he would be exhibiting those same stoic attributes so clear on Heung-min's face.

Heung-min glanced at Kane then, and offered the slightest of nods. He was okay, Kane realised. Kane nodded back, then continued searching the warehouse for any sign of inspiration, when he spotted something move from the corner of his eye and he shifted his gaze to the right. He saw a kind of recess nestled high in the wall, presumably where goods had at one time been lowered into or raised up from the ground level. Kane felt certain he had seen movement, but now all was still.

He wondered... *Jae-won?* But there was no further movement and he turned his eyes back towards Katashi.

"Okay, hang the boy upside down!" Katashi barked to the guards holding Heung-min.

Without warning, one of the men took a small baton from its holder on his belt and clubbed Heung-min on the base of his skull. Kane watched on with horror as the boy's lights went out and he crumpled to the floor. The guards then wrapped some packing straps around Heung-min's ankles, binding them together. Then one of the other men, using a remote controller, lowered the winch hook on its cable, and then looped the straps over the large steel hook. Using the controller again, the man slowly raised the hook and, inch by inch, Heung-min's inert body was hauled upside down until it came to a stop. His head swung two feet above the ground.

Thankfully, he was still unconscious for now and Kane looked on, totally helpless, as Heung-min's body swung gently from the hook.

"Please, Katashi, I beg you… don't do this… please, just let him go. Hang me there instead. I willingly offer myself over to you."

Katashi eyeballed Kane, his narrow grey eyes glaring at him with unbridled hatred. Yet that rage-filled expression then slipped away, replaced by something far worse from Kane's post of view. Katashi actually smiled. He was apparently enjoying himself, revelling in the sick horrors Heung-min was about to endure and of which Kane was sure he would be forced to witness and then probably the same suffer too.

Heung-min's body twitched subtly; he was coming around. Katashi stepped closer to his body and reached out with the blade, then drew it vertically down Heung-min's front, slowly, from waist to neck, slicing through the material of his shirt and ripping the fabric away, revealing the muscled torso beneath.

Then fixing his eyes on Kane, he rested the blade against Heung-min's stomach, pressing just hard enough to draw a thin line of blood.

Kane couldn't help himself, and launched his body

upwards, swivelling away from the guards behind him while still attached to the chair. But it was simply no use... the nearest guard just pushed hard into him and he fell clumsily onto his side, from where he looked up at the ceiling and roared in frustration.

There on one of the video feeds Jae-won saw his beloved son being strung up like a side of beef. Fire burned in his belly for what these cowardly bastards were doing and were about to do to Heung-min. Jae-won knew he had to act, and act fast. He analysed the scene before him. Kane was strapped to a chair. Half a dozen guards were standing around, all armed, and looking menacing.

There... Katashi Goto.

As a first impression, Jae-won was not impressed. The ancient man looked to be at least a hundred years old. He was short and stooped, and lean to the point of being emaciated. Yet Kane had told Jae-won of his nefarious deeds, and he knew he was not a man to be underestimated.

Jae-won scanned the rest of the live video feeds and, using his best judgment, he figured his best option was to try and get above the gathered bodies and take them by surprise. If he just burst in holding his acquired rifle, which he didn't really know how to use, he figured they would take him down in seconds.

He could not risk that. He *would* not risk it. He couldn't help his son if he himself was dead!

He hustled out of the monitoring room and made his way along a series of dark corridors until he found what he was looking for: a flight of stairs that led to the upper floors. So far he hadn't seen any more guards but he remained alert because he suspected it was only a matter of time until he did. Yet, he made it to his target, a wide hatch set into the wall above an old freight elevator, unseen by any of Katashi's goons.

He risked a glance around the corner into the warehouse below, and quickly pulled his head back. *Shit!* He thought he might have been seen. In the few seconds he had been looking, he saw Kane gazing in his general direction, and saw Katashi standing way too close to his son.

Jae-won took a few moments to compose himself and build up the courage to actually use the weapon he'd carried from down below. It was much heavier than he'd anticipated and he wondered if he could even get it to fire. He didn't want to kill anyone. In truth, whether they deserved it or not, he didn't even want to hurt any of the thugs, nor Katashi. That's not how Jae-won wanted to be, not like them, cruel, callous killers. He was raised better than that. Yet Jae-won knew that if it came to a simple choice between his son's life and Katashi Goto's, then the Japanese mob boss was as good as dead already.

Just then he heard a ruckus from the floor below, and risked a glance around the corner. Kane had seemed to have made some kind of attack, but was now being shoved to the ground, still attached awkwardly to the chair. Jae-won used the commotion to take aim and fire the rifle. He wasn't a gun user and had never before fired a weapon. He only wanted to cause a distraction, give Kane a chance to get free of the bonds. Yet somehow his shot found a mark and struck the guard nearest Katashi in the arm. He fell backward, more out of shock, it seemed, than any damage caused by the round.

The roar of the gun shot had all the guards scrambling for cover, their eyes frantically searching for the source of the attack, but they found no cover in the vast empty warehouse and Jae-won had ducked back out of sight before anyone had noticed him.

Katashi immediately—and wisely—stepped behind Heung-min's dangling body, knowing nobody would be foolish enough to risk injuring the boy. He knew he still had the upper hand as long as the boy was restrained on the winch, yet he silently cursed the guards he'd stationed at the doors and in the CCTV room. If they weren't dead already, he would make sure they were before this night was over.

Kane didn't need to look to know it was Jae-won who had fired the shot. He had seen that movement above moments before and had an inkling it was his friend. Kane used the momentary diversion to scramble to the nearest wall, difficult while still strapped to the chair. One guard followed him, gaining on him quickly, but just then the shooter fired a follow-up shot, and the bullet slammed into the concrete inches from the guard's feet, sending chunks of concrete shards and a cloud of dust into the air as the roar of the gun reverberated back at them all off the old brick walls.

The guard ceased his chase and ducked away, squeezing himself against the far wall of the warehouse, seeking cover with several of his comrades. Only Katashi remained in the centre of the space. Kane bustled to the opposite wall and slammed into what looked like a flimsy wooden door, which gave way under his weight and he found himself in a dark corridor. He acted swiftly.

Attached to the corridor wall was an ancient shelving unit, its metal framework affording Kane the chance to hack through his bonds by rubbing his proffered wrists against it. The rough, almost serrated edges of the frame made short work of the straps and in less than thirty seconds Kane's hands were free.

As he turned, he didn't even see the guard as the man aimed and fired, shooting Kane in the arm.

Chapter Forty-Eight

Luckily for Kane the bullet entered through the fleshy part of his lower arm and passed right out the other side. It had happened so fast he hadn't even felt it, but he had to act now as the man was shaping up to shoot him again and this time it probably wouldn't only hit his arm.

Kane grabbed the old shelf unit with both hands and pulled as hard as he could, and watched on as the hefty shelves toppled forwards. In the narrow corridor there was nowhere for the guard to run to. Kane had jumped backwards just in time to evade the falling unit and listened grimly as he heard the guard's bones breaking beneath the enormous weight of the steel-framed shelves.

Kane peered through the dust cloud that now filled the corridor. He stepped over and through the shelving to get closer to the guard and found him with one thin length of steel sticking up and out through his belly.

Well, that's unfortunate, Kane mused, but believed that if the guard didn't try and move himself, the injury probably wasn't life-threatening.

Now the immediate threat from the guard had passed, Kane had a chance to analyse his own wound. He saw a tiny hole on each side of his forearm, and blood trickled from both. It didn't hurt, yet, and Kane thought that if he wrapped it tightly he could wait to get it seen to professionally once this shit show was over.

"Hiram? Is that you?"

Kane spun at the sound of the voice and saw Jae-won emerge from the cloud of dust that had drifted off along the corridor.

"Jesus, what are you doing here?" Kane asked. "You should be at the hospital."

Jae-won ignored that comment. "We have to get to Heung-min… they are going to… we must…"

"Yes, we will. We have to be careful though. If we just burst in there now, they'll be waiting for us. We need to lure them out, pick them off one or two at a time."

Jae-won shook his head. "No!" he said flatly. "We cannot wait. I am going in now. I don't care what happens to me… I must help Heung-min."

Kane sighed. He knew Jae-won was right. If they waited, it might be too late. It was also akin to signing a death wish, considering who lay in wait back in the main warehouse. But there was no stopping Jae-won… he was going in there whether Kane liked it or not.

"Hold on a second," Kane said, turning away from Jae-won to check once more on the guard pinned beneath the shelving unit. "I think we can get closer to Katashi and Heung-min if we go in unarmed. If we have guns, I am certain they will simply shoot us. If we don't have guns their arrogance will not allow them to see us as a threat. We go in calmly and in peace, and when we get close enough, we take care of business. What do you say?"

Kane waited a couple of seconds, then spun around to look at Jae-won, who hadn't answered.

But his friend had already stepped out of the corridor and disappeared into the fray.

Chapter Forty-Nine

Several rounds zinged at Jae-won as he stepped into the warehouse, but none found their target and instead they slammed into the red-brick walls behind him, not too far from the doorway.

A moment later, Kane burst through behind Jae-won, ducking as shrapnel rained down all around. On seeing his friend's trajectory—straight towards Katashi and Heung-min, his weapon held out in front of him—Kane darted off in the other direction in order to split the cluster of the gun-toting attackers' target in half. A round screamed past his ear and thudded into the wall, spraying chips of brick and a small cloud of dust into the air.

He kept his head low and dived behind a stack of empty pallets a millisecond before a round thumped into the thick wood in the negative space his head had just vacated. He scrambled around to check on Jae-won and saw he had paused about ten feet short of his son hanging from the winch.

Katashi had the blade held tight against Heung-min's

Killing Koreana

throat. Kane saw that Heung-min was remaining passive, despite the very real threat against him. That was good. It meant Heung-min was biding his time, saving his energy for when his opponent made a mistake.

"You would be wise to stop there!" Kane heard Katashi say in English to Jae-won.

Even from his distance of perhaps thirty yards Kane could still see the turmoil etched on Jae-won's face. His friend was clearly raging and seemed to want nothing more than to shoot Katashi dead, then go to his son and help him down from the winch. Yet the madman had a blade against Heung-min's windpipe and Kane knew he would not hesitate to draw that blade across and kill Heung-min right before his father's eyes. He had willed Jae-won to stop and was relieved when he did. Kane saw Katashi nod.

What now? Kane wondered.

Katashi clearly held all the cards, despite Jae-won pointing a gun at him. They were outnumbered. They had only the one weapon, which Kane knew Jae-won wouldn't dare use in such proximity to his son, who was at the total mercy of a psychopath, his life hanging in the balance. Kane winced at the unfortunate turn of phrase.

What's our next move? Kane mused, shifting his gaze to the armed guards huddled over against the far left-hand wall. It was almost as if Katashi was toying with them. The old mob boss would have known Kane would come. He would have felt confident Kane would succeed in retrieving the Vase of Heaven. They already had the Tripitaka Koreana secured somewhere, maybe even in this facility. So why were they waiting? Kane had offered himself up to Katashi, but the former Yakuza don had refused, instead choosing to hurt Heung-min instead of Kane himself. Something didn't add up.

What the hell is Katashi's plan? Kane really needed to know.

Just then, the other guards all walked calmly towards Katashi in the centre of the warehouse, led by Kenji, who had a curious expression on his face Kane couldn't quite decipher. They too seemed to realise Jae-won wouldn't actually use the rifle he'd obviously taken from one of their colleagues at the entrance, and with nonchalance, two of them stepped right up to Jae-won, their own guns trained on him.

Katashi grinned and pushed the knife a little harder into Heung-min's skin. Jae-won flinched but the guards shoved him back with the barrels of their guns.

"Put down the gun!" Katashi continued in English, calmness personified. "Or I will slit his throat."

Kane couldn't quite see from that far, but he imagined Jae-won's nostrils flaring and his teeth grinding as he fought to control his rage, difficult, if not impossible in the face of such cowardly hostility. Kane was almost surprised when, after several beats, Jae-won lowered the rifle to the ground and nudged it away with his foot.

Katashi said, "That was a wise move. Now, on your knees."

"No. Please. Let my son go. He is just a—"

Jae-won didn't finish his sentence. The small yet solid baton collided with the back of his head at the same time as another rifle was swung hard against the backs of his knees. His legs buckled and he folded to the floor, but Jae-won was tough and Kane watched on in wide-eyed awe as the skilled warrior sprang to his feet. Yet before he could get in a strike of his own, a gun had seemed to appear from out of nowhere into Katashi's hands and he pressed it hard against

Heung-min's temple while the knife remained against the young man's neck.

Kane flinched, because he knew Katashi would not hesitate to inflict death upon the kid if Jae-won didn't back down. He looked on as Jae-won seemed to understand the gravity of the moment, and he raised his hands passively in the air and dropped to his knees, his head hung low and submissive. Kane was well aware how devastating that would have been for his friend. Yet, despite the escalating scenario, Kane felt sure it was a wise decision.

Bide your time. Let the other guy think they're in control. Do as they ask…

And when the moment comes that they drop their guard, even if for a split-second, be ready to take them down and deliver harsh justice upon them.

Chapter Fifty

With Heung-min still strung upside down on the winch and Jae-won now on his knees at the mercy of armed gangsters, Kane felt as if the situation had spiralled rapidly out of control. He himself was unarmed. He had an aversion for weapons of any kind and abhorred the use of guns. Yet, right now, as he crouched down behind the stack of pallets, his close friend and his friend's son in real danger of being murdered unceremoniously and without emotion by a madman and his thugs, Kane wished more than anything he had a weapon in his grasp. He was not a killer. Not a cold-blooded murderer like Katashi Goto. Yet it seemed sometimes as if the only way to defeat these monsters was to become a monster too.

Currently, that was literally no more than wishful thinking. Kane had nothing other than his wits and his athletic ability, both of which seemed to be useless to him in this dire predicament. In fact, the whole situation seemed beyond him. Somehow, they had walked into a living nightmare, and in that moment Kane oce more began to question his own value to the world. People who trusted him always got hurt. Sometimes, their fate was worse. Quite simply, people sometimes died because of him.

Kane felt a swell of anger churn in his stomach. It bubbled there for a moment before rising steadily through his system as he felt his knuckles clench and unclench and his teeth begin to grind. Kane had often been accused of possessing something akin to a death wish in the past, an accusation he found difficult to argue against at times, and it was a sense of that coming to him now, a notion that whatever he did could not resolve this situation, and in fact, would only make it worse.

Thus, there was nothing left for it but to put his own life on the line in a last desperate attempt to give Jae-won and Heung-min at the very least a fighting chance of survival.

He inhaled several deep breaths, composing himself for what he was about to do. He was going to charge Katashi and try to avoid dying for just long enough to get close enough to cut off the head of the snake.

Kane flexed his muscles, and with a last glance around the pallets before pushing off on what was almost certainly a suicide mission, he spotted movement at the far end of the warehouse. He hesitated, and when he realised what was on the pallet truck as it trundled and squeaked closer, he exhaled, sat back on his haunches, and waited.

The Tripitaka Koreana.

He watched as one of Katashi's goons wheeled the pallet containing the precious Korean cargo to the centre of the warehouse. Jae-won had been told by a contact in the police department that it was only approximately five percent of the ancient carved blocks that had been removed, but that still equated to around 4,000 of the beautifully crafted wooden blocks, and enough to render the collection incomplete. To some, it would not be that significant. Most of the collection remained undamaged, and it was still the single greatest of its kind anywhere in the world.

Yet to the Korean people, as attested to by Jae-won, it would feel as if their hearts had been ripped out, such was the vital cultural and historical significance to the nation of the famous *Tripitaka Koreana*. He recalled the words Jae-won had said to him back at the temple complex in Golgulsa just moments after they'd heard it had been stolen.

'When the spiritual soul of a nation is lost, its mortal death will surely follow.'

So when Kane saw the man who'd wheeled the stolen Tripitaka pieces in on the pallet truck reach down and pick up a huge jerry can and take off the lid, Kane knew Katashi meant to destroy it after all.

"Mister Kane, I think it is time you joined our little gathering." Kane didn't need to see who'd spoken to know the weak and wheezy words were said by Katashi; the words had carried to him clearly, due to the favourable acoustics of the cavernous warehouse.

Another voice addressed him now. He recognised it as Kenji. "If you do not come out of there now, we will destroy the Tripitaka. Then we will throw the bodies of your friends into the flames. You have ten seconds. Not a single second more!"

Kane closed his eyes. He had been about to attack the old man, ready to die to help his friends. Yet Katashi had beckoned him over. Perhaps a chance would present itself. Perhaps there could be a peaceful resolution after all. In truth, if he'd attacked the former Yakuza don, it would surely have been futile. The moment the guards saw him meaning to attack their boss, they would have gunned him down and his death would have been pointless. Whether that's what Kane deserved or not in the end mattered little to him now. He would serve no purpose to anyone dead.

Instead, if he played along, just maybe, Kane wondered, he'd even get an opportunity to end this drama in a manner Katashi himself might see fit… by making sure a dead man was actually dead.

Chapter Fifty-One

Kane now had two options.

Why the hell does it always come down to life or death choices?

This time, however, the choices were simple.

Either he disregarded Katashi's and Kenji's warnings, attack the old man anyway, and probably cause all the good guys to die.

Or, do as the old man asked, continue to play along, and even though he now suspected all the good guys would likely still die, he would at least have granted them a stay of execution, however short-lived that might be. Once again Kane winced as he realised his turn of phrase.

With the simple decision made, Kane stepped slowly out from behind the stack of pallets, raised his arms above his head and made his way cautiously towards the group in the middle of the warehouse. All was silent, other than the gentle thud of his footfalls on the concrete and the pulse hammering in his ears. The temperature seemed to have dropped, and Kane felt himself shiver as he made his way towards Katashi. As he walked, he noticed the bastard smirking.

Kenji stepped towards Kane, cutting off his progress. "Stop there!" Kenji demanded.

Kane did as he was told and waited while Kenji checked him for any concealed weapons. Kane briefly considered attacking the leader, and thought he could probably overcome him, yet that would only speed up his friend's demise, of that he was certain. So he ignored the burning desire to lash out and only smiled at Kenji when the man stood back from him and told him to proceed.

Kane continued his walk towards Katashi, Jae-won and the others, his darting eyes scanning the area for anything that might be of use or offer any hint of salvation.

"Stop!" Kenji demanded again, then the head thug went and stood beside Katashi.

Another guard then took the Vase of Heaven from Kane's backpack and approached the Tripitaka Koreana. He grinned at Kane, then looked towards Katashi, who nodded. The guard then tossed the ancient vase flippantly onto the pile of carved wooden blocks and Kane expected it to topple off and smash into a hundred small pieces. Somehow, however, the priceless artefact rolled back and forth a couple of times then settled, amazingly still in one piece.

What this showed Kane, with alarming certainty, was that Katashi really didn't give a shit about the financial value of the priceless artefacts, which must have been dozens of millions, given that the tiny Vase of Heaven alone was worth an alleged eight million dollars.

So, it is not about money. It is merely revenge. Then I really have nothing to lose.

He glanced at Jae-won, who had fixed his eyes upon Kane as he'd approached. Jae-won's expression was neutral and unreadable. Kane knew his friend would rather die than let these bastards get away with destroying the Tripitaka. But with Heung-min there, Jae-won would put his son's life above all else. Before the artefacts. Before his own life. *Definitely before my life.*

And Kane would do the same. He looked at his friend and offered him a sympathetic smile. "I love you, my brother," he declared for all to hear, and then he charged hard and fast at Katashi.

Kenji erupted from his position beside Katashi and with almost preternatural speed he flew in front of Kane and met him head on, the two physically-matched men colliding in a seismic crunch of jarring muscle and bone. They hit the concrete floor with a thud, each man grunting as they grappled to get a hold of the other's clothes.

The two hardened warriors writhed and struck out beneath the dim lights of the gloomy warehouse. The cold concrete beneath scraped at their bodies, as the other thugs and their weathered boss, Katashi, looked on with something akin to amusement.

Kenji was a formidable opponent, his muscles hard as iron and his grip determined as he clutched Kane's throat with one hand and jabbed him in the solar plexus with his other balled fist. Kane bucked and shimmied and managed to avoid the worst of the blows, and finally was able to connect with Kenji's jaw with a solid right elbow of his own. The Japanese thug momentarily lost his grip and Kane sprang to his feet fast, but even he was amazed at the speed with which Kenji also returned to a standing position.

Kane knew a martial arts expert when he saw one and knew Kenji had practiced the Judo he recognised for at least as long as he himself had practiced tae-kwon-do. Those decades of training made him a worthy adversary. Kane relished the challenge, as he suspected his opponent did also.

The two skilled fighters circled each other warily, each looking for an opening. Kane then made his first mistake. He had glanced at Jae-won, checking on his friend. His attention was diverted less than a second, and Kenji launched himself forwards with frightening speed, aiming a powerful kick at Kane's midsection. Kane's rigid torso absorbed the blow and he spun, then countered with a horrific left that collided with a forearm block by Kenji, though the force of Kane's blow sent the goon staggering back several steps.

Kane took a deep breath and regained his balance, his eyes never leaving Kenji's. He knew he couldn't afford to make any more mistakes against this dangerous adversary.

The two men traded several more vicious blows, their movements a blur of formidable strength and raw power. Kane's slight height advantage allowed him to get in a couple of powerful spinning kicks to Kenji's head, though none were debilitating, while Kenji's huge upper body granted him the strength to grab Kane and grapple him to the floor, just about getting Kane in a crushing, contest-ending headlock.

"Enough," barked Katashi, his voice finding a little strength. "This is not a pissing contest."

Kenji released Kane obediently yet with reluctance, then jumped to his feet and bowed slightly. Then, keeping one wary eye on Kane, he stepped away.

Kane rose cautiously and turned to face the former Yakuza don. What he saw then caused his heart to skip several beats.

Whilst absorbed in the fight, he'd failed to notice two of the guards had manhandled Jae-won over to the pallet containing the Tripitaka blocks, and tied his arms to the strapping that held the stacks of blocks in place.

Next to the Tripitaka stood Katashi. In his hands was a live flame, a bundle of rags wrapped around a two-foot-long wooden baton. The flames flickered and glowed in the gloom and cast wild shadows dancing across Katashi's face, making him appear like a living gargoyle.

Jae-won yelled to Kane, "Stay back. Do not try and—"

The nearest guard sent a devastating fist into Jae-won's kidneys and he fell silent. Kane flinched, ready to attack. Then, thinking better of it he quelled his rage and waited.

Kenji, still eyeballing Kane, then disappeared through a nearby door for a moment and when he returned, Kane's legs turned to jelly.

He approached Kane, and in both hands, he held aloft the very same samurai sword Katashi had once used to behead one of his own men.

Kane's eyes drifted towards Katashi, who smiled.

"I think it is time for us all to play a little game," he said.

Chapter Fifty-Two

"I'm tired of your fucking games, Goto," Kane retorted, once more using the old man's less formal surname. Being polite with a monster was apparently a waste of everyone's time.

"Now now, Mister Kane... now we are here in person, may I call you Hiram?"

Kane didn't answer.

"I am firmly of the belief that this is a game you should not only want to play, but that you must. There is too much at stake. However, if I am being honest, and as you might have already guessed, it is a game in which there can only be one winner. It will not be you."

"What a surprise!" Kane barked and almost chuckled. Yet with Jae-won and Heung-min still very much at the mercy of this deranged lunatic, he kept his misplaced amusement to himself.

Katashi smiled passively and nodded. "I understand your sarcasm. Nevertheless, Hiram, I think that despite our previous differences and, shall we say, our former conflicts, I believe that deep down you have to admit that I have displayed a certain level of respectfulness in our dealings. I only did what I had to do to survive on the island," he said, referring to their incidents on Miyajima. "As did you. And if I did not mention it before," he added, motioning to Kane's missing finger, "I am sorry about that. Though I do not expect forgiveness. Men like me… like us… do not need the sycophancy of other men."

"Men like us?" Now Kane was incredulous. "We are nothing alike, Goto. Nothing. You are nothing more than a narcissistic monster who has lost all sense of rationality. You should be in an asylum. Better yet, you should be dead!"

Kenji started to move towards Kane but Katashi halted him. "There is no need, Kenji," the old man said. "Hiram will come around to the idea of my game, you will see."

Kenji nodded. "Hai, Katashi-san," he said respectfully and stepped back, grinning at what he knew his boss had in store.

"So, a game, Hiram?"

What choice do I have? Kane mused, looking over at Jae-won strapped now to the top of the Tripitaka blocks, and at Heung-min still hanging upside down on the winch. Heung-min's eyes met his, and subtly the young man nodded, which Kane took as a sign that he was fine and ready for action if Kane could somehow get him down from the hook. This solidified Kane's belief that the kid was a warrior like his father, and that if the three of them could some how create the opportunity, they could indeed overcome these bastards, with or without weapons.

Kane glared at Katashi. "Okay, old man, what is this sick, depraved game of yours?"

Katashi grinned now, his face wrinkling like a dried prune. "Very good. Now Hiram, it is a simple game of choices. First, I will give you two options. Then, you must make a simple decision."

Kane didn't like the sound of this. Didn't like it one bit. "Go on."

The armed guards that stood around moved in a little closer, and it seemed to Kane most of them were unsure of what was about to transpire.

Katashi continued. "I know you are familiar with my sword. I know you know very well of what it is capable," he added with menace, despite the smile on his thin lips.

Kane would never forget what that sword had done and he felt a cold knot of realisation tightening in his guts.

No... please no, not that.

"Your two options, then. You will take the sword," Katashi said, wafting an arm towards Kenji, who held the sword at his side, its blade glimmering like diamonds under a full moon. "With that sword, you will remove the head of one of your two friends. The choice of which head to take is yours. However, failure to remove either head will result in the almost instantaneous deaths of all three of you. We will also pay a visit to that quaint little temple complex in the mountains... I hear the views are nice and the host is... welcoming. And not to mention, you will be responsible for the complete destruction of this pile of what these Koreans of yours believe to be important... artefacts, though to me they are nothing more than a collection of bits of dead trees some idiot once thought would look pretty carved with words. There is no accounting for taste when it comes to culture, now, is there Hiram?"

Kane seethed at the threats, but managed to speak. "I'd love to share some of my culture with you, Goto," Kane said, now sneering, and willing for just one chance to take the sword to the old man's neck.

Katashi ignored Kane's barbed remark. "So yes, failure to comply and you will all die, but not before a little fun and games at my behest," Katashi droned on. "I imagine being strapped down and burning slowly to death atop that pile of flaming wood would not be the most painless way to go, eh? So, is that clear, Hiram? Are you ready to play?"

In truth, Kane had expected something like this. The armed guards had moved in a little closer and now formed a tight, impenetrable circle around the proceedings. Several of them grinned. Only a couple remained unmoved, as if this was a regular kind of activity when Katashi Goto was involved. They all looked ready to do their bit to ensure their master got the result he desired.

Heung-min, who had remained silent this whole time, finally spoke from his position strung upside down beneath the shining steel winch.

"Hiram, it should be me," he said calmly. "I beg you, please, take the sword to *my* neck. The family needs my father to support them. They need him. They do not need me. Please, I *beg* of you." Despite the apparent desperate nature of the young man's words, they were spoken in a calm, calculated manner. Kane was suitably impressed.

"No!" bellowed Jae-won from his inert position strapped facedown against the ancient wooden blocks. "Hiram, listen to me. You do not harm my son. You hear me? Promise me, you bring that sword to my neck. Do not touch Heung-min."

Kane's eyes flicked between the two detained men, one a desperate father, the other a pleading son. Yet there was something in the younger man's words, something in the tone of his voice that belied the deadly predicament he was in. Kane was sure he heard pleading, but not pleading to be killed. It was a plea for Kane to pay greater attention to him.

Kane stepped closer to the gently swinging young man. He watched as Heung-min shimmied a little, his weight interplaying with gravity and causing him to spin a half turn, just enough that Kane noticed he had somehow gotten his hands free of the bonds that had tied them together. Heung-min kept his two hands close, but on both hands his thumb and forefingers formed the universal sign for okay, a gesture apparently missed by everyone else in the warehouse.

Kane was amazed. He had no idea how Heung-min had managed it, but it gave Kane a massive surge of both pride, and confidence.

This shit is not over yet. Not by a long fucking shot.

"Hiram, please, no... listen to me," Jae-won begged and Kane pitied the man who believed his son was about to be beheaded by a friend. Kane could only wonder at the inner turmoil Jae-won must have been enduring in that moment, and his heart ached for the proud father.

Kane approached Katashi and Kenji. Kenji held out the sword, as a few of the watching guards raised their weapons and trained them on Kane's head as he moved.

"I have made my decision," he said.

The old man nodded, unable to keep the sick joy from his withered face. Kane was repulsed by the sight of the old man, revelling in causing such misery to others. Kane met his gaze, and saw in them darkness, hatred and cold, callous indifference to their suffering.

Kane reached out for the sword from Kenji, but the Japanese thug held onto it as Kane pulled. "Do not try anything, or I promise you, everyone you have ever loved will suffer."

Kane ignored the threat and nodded. Kenji released the sword and Kane took it, feeling its weight in his hands. The heft of it surprised him and he recalled the ease with which Katashi had wielded it all those years ago. He would struggle to handle it as well as the old man had then.

"Jae-won, Heung-min is right," Kane said quietly to his friend, who upon hearing those words began to thrash and rage against the straps holding him to the pallet.

"No, please, I beg you. Kill me, Hiram," the distraught man wailed, agony lacing his words. "Kill me and save Heung-min."

"I am sorry, my friend, the finest friend and mentor a man could ever wish to have. But I must kill Heung-min."

With that, and ignoring the desperate screams of his old friend Jae-won, Kane whispered "Sorry" one last time, then turned and, with his muscles tensing under the strain, and his heart pounding beneath his ribs, he swung the mighty samurai sword in a wide, high and graceful arc towards the upside-down Heung-min's neck.

Chapter Fifty-Three

It was as if it were all happening in slow motion.

The watching thugs and their leader Kenji had frozen solid with anticipation of that was about to transpire. They had all lowered their weapons, each of them distracted to the point of negligence as they waited for Kane to deliver the killing blow.

Jae-won's desperate wailing had ceased as he tried in vain to block out the world and recede into his own mind, his eyes screwed shut and nausea threatening to spill as bile burned his throat like toxic acid.

Katashi Goto, the mastermind of the sick, depraved tableau, had his small eyes opened wide, sparkling with expectation. His lips were moist and his weak heart sped up just a little as he watched with morbid glee as Kane turned towards the young man hanging upside down from the hydraulic winch.

Heung-min himself felt at peace as he regulated his breathing, taking short breaths and exhaling quickly, in time with his heartbeat. He sensed a shadow approaching on the concrete floor two feet beneath his head, growing as the space around him darkened as Kane moved closer... as he moved to within striking distance. Heung-min flexed his fingers and wrists, readying himself for whatever might happen next. He believed Kane understood what he'd meant with the 'okay' symbols he'd displayed with his fingers and thumbs. Now he was moments from finding out. If he'd misread the situation, he would be dead in less than three seconds and nothing would matter anymore.

Kenji gazed at the head of the man hanging from the winch as Kane turned towards him. Fascinated by what he was about to witness—he'd heard of Katashi's sick games before, but this was his first up-close and personal experience of it—he felt a surge of adrenalin as Kane began to swing the samurai sword, though at the last second, he noticed the man's hands twitching, slowly moving apart from each other; it took mere milliseconds for Kenji to realise the implications...

"Stooopppp!" he yelled.

Kane took a final deep breath and raised the sword, and with all the force he could muster he swung it towards the head of his friend's son. Yet at the very final moment he arched his back, and as the sword began levelling out and finally going upwards instead of down, he screamed and crashed the deadly blade into the chains with a metallic crunch mere inches above Heung-min's elevated feet.

It was too late, and by the time Kenji had uttered his futile demands Kane had sliced through the chains, freeing the prisoner.

The hefty steel chains were no match for the wild aggression with which Kane had swung the sword and against the odds, they yielded with ease. Heung-min had readied himself in case he'd read the situation right, and as he fell, he thrust his arms downwards and braced against his impact with the concrete below, potentially preventing a broken neck. Like a cat, he landed softly and immediately rolled to his left and sprang to his feet.

Kane used the momentum of the massive swing to swing again, and as he surged towards the nearest guard he brought the sword down once more, severing the man's arm at the elbow; the forearm, the hand and the gun it contained flew across the space, spraying blood out in a fine mist. The man collapsed screaming to the floor.

Katashi looked on in a mix of rage and fascination as Kane and Heung-min took the fight to the stunned guards. He had long known Kane to be a worthy adversary, but even the former Yakuza overlord had underestimated the Englishman this time. Despite all that was raging around him, Katashi remained calm and stepped closer to Jae-won, who was still face down against the blocks of the Tripitaka, and who was yet to realise what had happened.

Without a second's hesitation, Katashi placed his flaming torch on the ground and, with no little effort, hoisted the heavy jerry can full of gasoline and began pouring it over the ancient Korean artefacts, making sure to douse the trussed Korean man as well. He was smiling as he did it.

As the gasoline splashed into Jae-won's face, Jae-won's head shot backwards. The fuel burned his eyes and he immediately realised what was happening. He yelled out, but some of the noxious liquid splashed into his throat and he vomited onto the wooden blocks in front of him.

Kenji darted around the pallet containing the winch

and, just as Kane was about to bring the sword down on another of the armed guards—it was the woman, who was struggling to raise her gun in time—with tremendous force he slammed his shoulders into the back of Kane's legs. The momentum barrelled Kane forwards and inadvertently, Kenji had hastened the woman's demise as the sword came down directly onto the top of her head, cleaving away half her skull and taking chunks of her face, brain and tissue with it. The woman fell silently to the floor, dead instantly and lying now in a dark, spreading slick of her own blood.

Heung-min had managed to find himself faced with two guards, who had thrown down their guns and came at him together, crouched in fighting stances with their arms raised out in front. The two men prowled, sending out devastating jabs in a lopsided game of cat and mouse. Heung-min was stiff from his time strung upside down and as the blood returned to his legs, he felt pins and needles burn like daggers. Yet he was young and in supreme shape, and soon recovered, dodging the incoming strikes with relative ease as the bulkier, slower men tried in vain to land with their shots. Frustrated, one of the men growled and lunged wildly, but he slipped and Heung-min lashed with out a straight-legged kick, connecting directly in the centre of the man's shin. The audible crack of the tibia was music to his ears as the huge man screamed and went down, clutching at his destroyed leg.

Now one on one, Heung-min relaxed into the duel, confident it was only a matter of time until the Japanese thug made a similar mistake.

Kane had dropped the sword and spun on his heels to face the advancing Kenji, who now grinned as he closed in on Kane, who backed up a little, edging around towards the winch. The broken chains still swung lightly under their own weight, the steel hook glinting with menace from the floor. Kenji swung a lightning fast right cross which Kane parried, then responded with a devastating left upper cut that landed a glancing blow on Kenji's chin that didn't cause any damage but was enough for the smile to be replaced by a sneer.

Kenji then launched suddenly from a standing position and flashed out a scissors kick which Kane anticipated and, with innate deft agility, he somehow avoided the powerful kick, and with his right arm swung hard, connecting perfectly with the foot and making Kenji topple to his right and crash to the concrete floor. Kane pounced and piled in with a blur of ferocious punches and knees to Kenji's exposed back and shoulders, but Kenji was strong and somehow withstood the attack. He managed to scramble to his feet, ready to face off with Kane again, who couldn't help but admire the man's strength and resilience.

The two warriors circled, waiting for the perfect moment to strike, both well aware that they had met their fighting match. For both men it was the very first time.

Katashi stood behind Jae-won and retrieved a handkerchief from his pocket, then proceeded to wipe the Korean man's eyes.

"Your son is a tough warrior," Katashi said. "It is a shame he will watch you burn."

Jae-won thrashed against the bonds that detained him against the pallet but it was no use. He was simply strapped too tightly. The struggle caused another bout of vomiting and Katashi stepped back to avoid it getting on his shoes.

He glanced over at the two separate battles going on. He considered just picking up one of the discarded semi-automatic weapons and simply shooting everyone... including Kenji and his own remaining men... but that was too easy. He wanted Kane and the young man to watch this Korean dog die… wanted to see what they would do.

He relit the torch that had extinguished and watched as the flame grew, and casually stepped closer to the pallet of Tripitaka blocks.

Chapter Fifty-Four

Jae-won had turned his head and now realised with burgeoning horror what was about to happen. "Heung-min!" he yelled as loud as he could, despite the acidic burning in his throat. "Hiram!"

Yet his pleas fell on deaf ears as Kane and Heung-min continued to fight their combatants in a blur of arms and legs. His weak voice couldn't cut through the noise of the fight and he screamed internally as his real voice faded to nothing more than a croaked whisper.

"It is okay," Katashi told him in English. "They will come soon. Will it be soon enough?"

With that, the grinning, psychotic former mafia don dropped the flaming torch on top of the gasoline-doused pallet loaded with the four thousand priceless carved blocks of the Tripitaka Koreana.

The blocks were carved from hard wood and didn't ignite easily. However, the straps holding them down and the gasoline did. After a mere second, there came an almighty *whoomph* as the gas exploded, the flames roaring upwards a dozen feet in seconds.

The roar of the explosion caught the attention of everyone in the warehouse, who all spun to face the inferno suddenly raging before them. Kane and Heung-min realised immediately what the fire meant, and abandoned their individual battles to race to Jae-won's rescue. Kane glanced at Katashi as he sprinted to the fiery stack and saw the madman chuckling to himself. It was then Kane vowed, in that very instant, that he could not allow the monster to leave the building alive.

Kenji had chased the two men as they'd hurried desperately towards their friend and father, wanting to prevent them helping the splayed out Korean. But Katashi signalled to him to back off, so Kenji came to stand beside his boss and the two men watched on with increasing satisfaction as Kane and Heung-min struggled to help Jae-won.

Jae-won's voice had quit altogether but as yet the flames hadn't reached his edge of the pallet. Heung-min arrived and grabbed his father around the waist, yanking back hard and struggling desperately to pull him away from the pallet of burning blocks as thick black smoke swirled and twisted like slow-moving tornados towards the ceiling of the warehouse high above. Kane searched frantically for a knife to cut the straps which were burning ever closer to Jae-won's arms, but none were in sight and he felt bereft as the flames crept within inches of his friend's extended arms.

Smoke now drifted all around, making visibility in the warehouse limited, and he remained alert incase Kenji decided to sucker punch him from within the gloom.

The sword…

Kane abandoned his search for a knife and cursed himself for not thinking of the sword sooner, but he watched on in growing horror as the flames began licking at Jae-won's fingers and then engulfed his hands and forearms too.

Jae-won's struggles ceased as he fell into delayed shock with the relentless pain, and Heung-min roared in distraught frustration as the flames spread across his father's head and neck and the exposed skin began to bubble and blister before his eyes.

Kane and Heung-min's eyes met and the two distraught men seemed to have arrived at the same horrific conclusion; Jae-won couldn't be saved, but he could be spared any further agony. Even if they could somehow douse the flames, it was too late for Jae-won, so they had to do the right thing. As unimaginable as the decision was, they had to end Jae-won's suffering…

Inexplicably, Katashi had retrieved the sword himself and now flung it at their feet before backing away to safety on the other side of the fire. Kane stooped down and grabbed it up and made ready to take the unthinkable decision to actually terminate his friend's life in order to end his agonised pathway to death.

"No, I will do it," Heung-min stated flatly, grim determination in his eyes as he grabbed the sword from Kane's hands before Kane could react.

"No, Heung-min, it should not be—" Kane started to protest but a stern look from the young man told him it was futile. Kane nodded and stepped back from the inferno as Heung-min did what no person should ever have to endure.

"Appa salang hae-yo," he said. "Mian hae-yo." *I love you father. I am sorry.*

Heung-min roared in anger and utter devastation and rage and brutal, infinite torment as he swung the sword down onto his father's flaming neck, liberating his head from his shoulders and killing him instantly as the flames whooshed at his own shirtless torso, threatening to consume him too. Heung-min discarded the deadly sword into the inferno and staggered back, dropping to his knees, but Kane hauled him up to his feet and away from the towering fire that had now swallowed the entire stack of Tripitaka blocks in a maelstrom of swirling flames, and had now engulfed Jae-won's head and body completely.

Through a momentary gap in the flames, across on the other side of the fire, Kane saw Katashi Goto standing there with a small, smirking smile on his sadistic face. There was no sign of Kenji.

Too late Kane saw movement from the corner of his eye as Kenji attacked from the left and delivered a stunning right cross that rattled Kane's jaw and staggered him backwards towards the winch. Kane recovered fast, now existing on pure hatred and adrenalin as he turned to face Kenji.

Heung-min had risen to his feet and like a zombie, and walked slowly around the perimeter of the fire towards his nemesis and the man who had caused his father's agonising death. The one remaining guard saw this and raced to his boss's side, grabbing a gun from the floor on his way. Katashi's smile remained fixed as the guard stepped between his boss and the approaching Heung-min, who had only one thing on his mind: justice.

"Stop!" demanded the guard, but Heung-min ignored him and walked directly at the gun. The guard pulled the trigger. Nothing happened. The thug then checked the safety and grinned like a lunatic as he clicked the safety off and raised the gun again and fired. On pure instinct Heung-min ducked and the round missed, and Heung-min unleashed a right upper cut that started down by his knees and connected with the thug's jaw, breaking it in several places and knocking him out cold. The huge man crumpled to the floor and Heung-min followed up with a devastating kick that connected so hard with the thug's temple that even above the roar of the flames Heung-min heard the bastard's neck break.

Heung-min turned to Katashi Goto. This time, as Katashi's smile faltered Heung-min's own soot-blackened face erupted in a grin, and it was the maniacal grin of a young man on the edge of madness.

Chapter Fifty-Five

Kenji growled as Kane launched himself once more at the Japanese thug, who seemed surprised at Kane's high-level of fighting ability and the way he continued going at him with relentless energy. Truthfully, Kane's physical energy had waned but it was the unparalleled hatred he now felt towards Kenji and Katashi and all the world that empowered him forwards with growing intensity time and time again.

This time Kane's right cross connected solidly with Kenji's chin and wobbled him, but he recovered swiftly and countered with a combination of lefts and rights of his own, walking Kane backwards against a brick wall of the warehouse. Kane ducked and weaved, and when Kenji lost balance momentarily Kane thrust a knee upwards into the man's groin area and Kenji doubled over, winded as Kane seized the moment and forced Kenji upright, swinging a destructive right hook into the side of his head, followed by a thunderous left and another right upper cut.

Kenji's vision clouded and he staggered backwards,

almost losing his footing as he approached the centre of the vast space. Behind him, the fire grew ever more rampant and Kane noticed the flames had even reached the wooden support beams of the ceiling, licking the underside of the roof and threatening to engulf the entire dilapidated building.

Over Kenji's shoulder Kane saw they were approaching the winch and he recalled seeing the giant steel hook that he'd severed from its chains. It gave him an idea.

Heung-min had lost all sense of reality as he stalked towards a backward-stepping Katashi. He knew the deranged former mob boss could no longer fight. Nor could he run. Heung-min darted around the old man and turned their direction back towards the fire that had now reached the ceiling fifty feet above and had engulfed the ancient timbers that held up the roof. Bits of flaming wood and asbestos began to rain down around them, but Heung-min ignored it all and, even when Katashi grinned and removed a small pistol from his pocket and pointed it at his chest, he did not desist from his path and kept forcing Katashi Goto back towards the inferno.

"It is a shame it has to end this way," Katashi said, his voice barely discernible over the roaring flames. "You would be a valuable asset. Oh well," he added, then fired the gun from eight feet away into Heung-min's advancing body.

Almost as if Heung-min hadn't felt the round enter his right arm, he marched onwards, closing in on Katashi, who squinted amid the swirling smoke and fired again. This time the round dealt Heung-min's shoulder a glancing, grazing blow then continued by more or less harmlessly. The next bullet clipped his hip and Heung-min ignored the flare of pain and surged forwards as if in a trance and as if commanded forth by an unseen master of puppets.

Panicked now, Katashi backpedaled, unleashing the rest of the rounds and hoping one or more of the bullets would deliver death unto this new nemesis. With the clip now empty of all eight bullets Katashi was horrified to see the young man still advancing like a ghostly wraith through the eddying smoke. He scanned the wild, dystopian scene for any sign of Kenji and salvation but saw nothing but crazed dancing shadows and slain bodies. Then he risked a glance over his shoulder and saw the fire just a dozen feet behind him.

Kenji sensed something in Kane's eyes as he stumbled and tried to keep his balance as he staggered backwards, but the smoke had dispersed across the entire warehouse floor and visibility was down to mere feet. Still Kane came at him, and Kenji knew he had to do something drastic, something to halt Kane's dominance.

Without warning, he dropped to the ground and rolled to one side, hoping to spring up amid the smoke and catch Kane unaware. But Kane was quick, too quick for Kenji, and reacted on instinct, stooping low and administering a sickening straight-armed cross to Kenji's chin as Kenji rose to meet him.

Kane saw the whites of Kenji's eyes as they rolled back in his head and knew it was game over for Katashi's head thug. Just a few feet away on the concrete floor Kane spotted the steel hook from the winch, illuminating its presence to him as it reflected the muted orange/yellow glow of the dancing flames beyond. The hook had come to rest against the edge of the pallet holding the winch, its long, curved end sticking upwards.

Nodding to himself, as if to convince himself his next action was justified, Kane reached down and grabbed Kenji by the scruff of his military fatigues and shuffled him towards the hook. When he was within reach, Kane inhaled, and with the last of his dwindling strength he lifted Kenji's limp body two feet in the air, and as the cold-blooded killer's eyes opened and glared at Kane, and his mouth curved into a sneer, Kane let gravity do its business and he released his grip on Kenji, who fell back onto the hook, which pierced straight into his back and protruded out through his sternum. Kenji's lifeless eyes stared unseeing at Kane and the crooked sneer on his lips would remain fixed there for all eternity.

Kane exhaled, blinking to clear the stinging smoke from his eyes, and turned in time to see Heung-Min through a brief break in the cloying smoke.

"No," he yelled as he saw what Heung-min was about to do, and he raced over, already knowing it was too late.

Heung-min smashed the gun out of Katashi's weak hand and shoved him backwards, now dangerously close to the raging fire.

"There is still a way out of this," Katashi pleaded, his final lame, desperate words falling on indifferent ears.

"No," was all Heung-min said. "Not this time."

He shoved Katashi again, and then once more, until the old man slammed against the edge of the pallet of Tripitaka blocks, consumed by flames and slowly being reduced to worthless ash.

"Please," Katashi said, "I beg you," he muttered pathetically and raised his hands in front of him in the universal symbol for prayer, yet his prayers went unanswered as Heung-min grinned at Katashi and grabbed both his hands. Then he shoved.

"For my father," Heung-min said as Katashi toppled backwards into the fire that he himself had started and in seconds was engulfed by flames that licked and swirled around his frail arms and legs and his head erupted and his eyeballs popped and his skin blistered and peeled away, and then the old man was gone and it was all over.

Chapter Fifty-Six

Kane spun Heung-min around to face him. He was met with a vacant, haunted look on the young man's face and though Kane believed Katashi deserved to die for all that he had done over five decades of brutal crimes and inhumanity, and for all the pain and suffering he had inflicted on countless victims in his half-century-long reign of terror, it should have been Kane who'd administered those last rites.

Yet he understood why Heung-min had acted as he had. His father's death was solely down to Katashi's insanity, and yet it has been Heung-min himself who'd delivered the final blow. Kane wondered if the courageous young man would ever get over it, and vowed there and then that he would offer Heung-min and his family whatever support they needed and for however long they needed it.

There was no time to dwell on that now as a huge timber beam crashed from the ceiling in flames just thirty yards away, followed by a huge sheet of burning asbestos that disintegrated as it hit the concrete.

"Heung-min, we have to go!" Kane yelled over the now

deafening roar of the fire and massive chunks of debris crashing to the concrete floor.

Heung-min stared blankly at him, as if in a daze. Kane knew the signs of shock all too well and without warning, he slapped Heung-min hard across the cheek.

Heung-min blinked and stared at Kane, slowly registering his friend in front of him. He blinked a couple more times and Kane saw Heung-min coming back to him as another huge beam crashed down, this one even closer.

"We have to get out of here now!" Kane bellowed, and Heung-min nodded.

Kane grabbed his arm and they turned and trotted towards the far end of the building where the doors stood open, doors through which the now destroyed Tripitaka had been brought just thirty minutes earlier.

They hustled through and darted along a dark corridor, smoke drifting lazily along the dim passage. Kane led them around a corner and there they spotted a door which Kane hoped led to the outside. The door was locked with a rusted padlock that appeared as if it hadn't been used in decades. Kane took a weary step back, and with his muscles burning, he unleashed a kick powerful enough to liberate the padlock from its clasp. He slung open the creaking door and the two men stepped out into the small hours of the morning.

The snow from earlier had ceased falling but now lay in deep swathes across what was probably an unused carpark for the now abandoned warehouse's former staff. The icy temperature felt good after the heat of the interior and the men laboured through the snow and away from the warehouse.

The sound of wailing sirens gave them pause and Kane pulled them into the doorway of a boarded-up shop. They turned to face the old warehouse and saw flames erupting into the black sky, casting an eerie, apocalyptic glow across the entire area. The sirens approached, probably less than two minutes away, and were likely a combination of police, fire engines and ambulances.

"How are your wounds?" Kane asked, looking at the blood that had soaked into Heung-min's jeans.

"I'll be fine," Heung-min replied honestly. In truth, the wounds individually were not serious, but combined, it was obvious they spelled danger.

Appraising Heung-min's shirtless body, Kane understand how lucky he'd been and knew he needed professional medical help soon. He nodded. "Let's get out of here."

Kane set off at a trot, but noticed Heung-min hadn't followed and he stopped and walked back to the young man.

"Katashi Goto got what he deserved," Heung-min said.

Kane nodded.

"My father deserved much better," Heung-min added simply, gazing back at the now collapsing old brick-built warehouse. "He did not deserve to die that way."

"No, he did not," Kane said. Gazing back at the inferno bringing down the warehouse one brick and one flaming beam at a time, Kane offered up a silent prayer to a god he knew wasn't listening and thought of Jae-won, the bravest most humble man he had ever known. "No, he did not."

With that, the two men jogged away and turned a corner out of sight just as the first police car raced towards the warehouse from the other end.

And then they were gone, two living ghosts in a night full of horrific and senseless death.

Epilogue

Kane made his way along the hospital hallway. The harsh glare of the overhead lighting cast a stark contrast against his shadowed face. The air was heavy with the scent of antiseptic as he walked with purpose, his footsteps padding lightly against the linoleum floor as he approached the private room in which Heung-min lay recovering from his multiple injuries.

A lone policeman stood outside Heung-min's door, and he eyeballed Kane as he came to a stop in front of him. Kane offered a polite bow, which was half returned by the younger police officer, more out of his Confucius beliefs, Kane thought, than politeness. The officer resumed his sentry duty without a word.

Kane paused for a few moments, glancing through the window and looking at Heung-min, who seemed to be dozing peacefully. Kane waited another minute, then entered. Heung-min lay motionless in the bed except for the gentle rise and fall of his strong chest. The skin of his face was pale, other than the bruises and inflamed swelling around his eyes.

Pushing open the door, Kane was met with the soft chimes and the whirrs of the machines surrounding the young man, a multitude of wires and tubes protruding from various parts of his bandaged arms and chest. Kane trod carefully towards the bed and silently carried a chair to sit closer to the stricken kid. Despite Kane's attempts to be quiet, Heung-min stirred at his presence. Grimacing as a surge of pain swept through his body, Heung-min's eyes sparkled as he greeted his friend with a weak smile.

Kane forced a smile in return, though he was heartsick for what, in part, he had caused to befall this brave young man.

Kane's voice was low and solemn as he asked, "How are you feeling?" Kane shook his head. "Sorry, that was a stupid question."

Heung-min managed a half smile. "Better... better than I was yesterday," he said, his voice little more than a breathy whisper. "Thanks for..." He paused to inhale, then coughed a few times, his face screwing up in pain. Once recovered, he said, "Thank you for coming."

Kane sat down on the bony plastic chair and gazed at his old friend's courageous son, fighting back tears that threatened to betray his emotions. The doctor had told him during yesterday's visit that Heung-min had suffered some second degree burns to his arms, though they were expected to heal fully. The two bullets he had taken, one in his chest, and another in his arm, had been removed, though it was lucky they were low-caliber bullets. A third bullet had taken a chunk of skin from a hip, but there should be no lasting damage with any of the wounds, the doctor added, and no infections had taken hold. Smoke inhalation had affected

Heung-min's breathing, but again, within a day or two any lingering effects of that should have passed.

"All in all," the doctor had informed Kane, "this young man has been very, very lucky."

No shit, Kane mused but didn't say. *If only his father…*

Kane shook off thoughts of his slain friend Jae-won for now and focused on his mentor's son.

"The doctor tells me you should be out of here in a week. What will you do?"

"Mother thinks I should stay home. My uncle is coming to stay at the temple complex for a few weeks to help out. I don't know… I want to go back to university."

"Your mother is right," Kane said. "At least for a little while. They will need you there, Heung-min. You're the man of the house now…" Kane turned his head away from Heung-min, in a vain effort to hide his own anguish.

"It's not your fault, Hiram," Heung-min said, sensing Kane's troubled mind. "None of it is your fault."

Kane inhaled and cuffed a few stray tears away with his jacket sleeve. *How can he say that? How can he be so forgiving, despite everything that's happened and what he was… what he felt he had to do?*

An image of Heung-min with the sword in his hands standing over the burning body of his father was something Kane knew he would never be able to erase from his mind. He only hoped Heung-min would embrace the psychiatric counselling and support he had already received and was surely going to need more of over the coming weeks and months, and probably for the rest of his life. No human should have to endure what Heung-min had been through. Especially not in the way things had transpired.

He glanced at Heung-min now, whose eyes had closed as he suffered a fresh wave of pain. His heart went out to the brave young man. Kane knew he wouldn't be able to put on such a stoic façade had the tables been turned. Kane himself had suffered only minor injuries and had somehow avoided inhaling any damaging amounts of the noxious smoke in the warehouse.

He reached out and gently grabbed Heung-min's hand. "I am so very sorry for your loss, Heung-min. Your father was a good man... a great man. The best I've ever known. I will miss him."

Heung-min didn't say anything, but Kane felt him squeeze his hand tight. And that was enough. It was much, much more than Kane could expect from the son of the man he had led to his death.

Kane stood up from the seat and turned to leave, but stopped. Standing at the window outside the room was Heung-min's mother, Jae-won's heartbroken wife, Ju-hye. Kane offered a small bow and made his way to the door and stepped outside Heung-min's room.

"I... I don't know what to say, Ju-hye. My words could never express how devastated I am and how sorry I am for what has... for what happened to Jae-won. It—"

Ju-hye placed a hand on Kane's forearm. Her skin was cold as she held it there firmly, her gaze fixed onto Kane's eyes.

He expected her to unleash her vitriol upon him and Kane understand it is what he deserved. Instead she closed her eyes and inhaled, then said:

"Thank you for helping bring my boy back. I... my family is grateful to you."

Kane wanted to protest, wanted to tell Ju-hye that if it weren't for him, Jae-won would be alive and Heung-min wouldn't have almost lost his life too. Yet, deep down, far past the place where reason did battle with his conscience,

Kane wasn't sure if that was the truth. He hadn't kidnapped Heung-min. He hadn't caused Katashi Goto to come back into his life and enter into theirs. Kane didn't steal the Tripitaka, and he hadn't demanded anyone steal the Vase of Heaven. Jae-won would have gone on to Daegu without Kane, of that there was no doubt.

Looking into his friend's wife's eyes now, Kane knew Ju-hye understood that too.

Ju-hye gazed past Kane at her son lying motionless on the hospital bed. She let her eyes drift to the series of tubes that crisscrossed his body, and then looked at the machines that kept his breathing regulated and monitored his vital signs. Then she looked back at Kane. Without another word, she reached up and kissed him on the cheek, and Kane thought it was the kindest, bravest and most welcome gesture he could ever have imagined.

"Gam-sa hap-nida," was all Kane could manage. "Thank you."

Ju-hye let Kane go and placed one hand on the door to Heung-min's room, then paused. She did not turn to look at Kane, and kept her eyes on her son as she said, "It is so difficult to see the future when everything feels so very uncertain now. Heung-min will recover. The doctor has assured me of it. Ji-yeon will miss her father. I will miss my husband and my best friend."

Kane watched as Ju-hye battled against her emotions, inhaling and exhaling gently. He had never met a more stoic woman than Ju-hye. Finally, she glanced back at Kane.

"Don not be a stranger," she said, and they were the most humbling words Kane had ever heard.

Kane watched as Ju-hye entered the room and went to sit by her son, as Kane had done before. He looked on as she too took one of Heung-min's hands in both of hers, and pressed the back of it to her lips. And then she sobbed, and it was all Kane could do to prevent his own tears from streaming as he left the hospital and stepped out into a bitterly cold winter's day.

Kane stood alone in silence on the front steps of the small yet beautiful main temple at the Golgulsa complex in the mountains near the eastern coast.

It had been almost two weeks since the dénouement of those traumatic events, first in Gyeongju and then later, tragically, in Daegu. Kane had been advised by the police of both cities to stay in the province for the time being, although he had decided to remain for a further few weeks anyway. He wanted to be on hand for Jae-won's family for whatever they needed. He had played a part in the drama happening to begin with, albeit inadvertently. He would take an active part in the family's healing process too, for as long as they needed him, or for as long as he felt welcome.

After a series of interviews by the respective police forces, as well as character witness statements from Jae-won's family, Nam-gil, the security guard at Gyeongju National Museum—who Kane learned had helped Jae-won escape the museum and then taken him to Daegu—had testified that Kane had done no wrong, other than trying to help rescue his friend's son. Kane was a hero, in Nam-gil's eyes, as was Jae-won, he told the authorities, and he pleaded on both men's behalf that they were innocent of any wrong doing.

Ultimately, the police had decided to release Kane without charge. In fact, they had used Kane's own testimony to identify and name all of the dead bodies uncovered at the collapsed, burned-out warehouse in downtown Daegu. Among them were half a dozen Japanese gangsters, including their leader, Kenji Omaru, a known former special forces military operative-turned-freelance gangster and assassin, and a man wanted for multiple murders in his own country, as well as here in the Republic of South Korea.

The Korean police had wanted to reward Kane for helping bring these criminals to justice. He had politely declined. He also kept the incidents with the winch hook and the samurai sword firmly to himself.

There had also been the unidentifiable remains of an older male. Kane had considered informing the police it was Katashi Goto, but decided against it. He wasn't entirely certain why he'd opted to play ignorant regarding Katashi, but guessed it was probably selfish. If he had revealed his knowledge that it was indeed the former Yakuza overlord, a man who had been considered dead for several years, then the questions would have kept on coming, and Kane had neither the desire nor the will to prolong this latest nightmare. He had thought Katashi Goto dead once. Now he knew it was an undeniable truth; that was more than enough for Kane.

There had been some uneasy tension around the temple complex for the first week or so as Ju-hye had struggled to come to terms with what had happened, but in the last couple of days she had treated Kane well and with compassion, despite her own heartbreak. Kane knew she understood he had almost lost his life too, and that after speaking with her son, Heung-min had told Kane he'd assured his mother Kane had done everything he could to help and that he should not be shunned. She had known it in her heart, Heung-min told him, and that was now showing through in her actions.

Kane shrugged his broad shoulders tighter into his jacket to ward off the biting chill as fat snowflakes drifted around him like confetti tossed at a winter wedding. The temple, a place of serenity and contemplation, was a perfect refuge for a man haunted by the events of recent times. He had come here every day since his return to Golgulsa, often multiple times a day, and it was helping to sooth his angst and focus on his own mental healing.

There had been some good news. He'd had a conversation with the director of the temple complex at Haeinsa, home of the Tripitaka Koreana. Such was the consistency of the wood, and the effects of hundreds of years of dedicated treatment of the estimated four-thousand ancient carved blocks that had been stolen and set on fire in the warehouse, less than three-hundred had been damaged beyond repair. A couple of hundred more could be treated and salvaged, and work was already well underway. The rest of the priceless blocks were more or less unharmed, which to Kane, having witnessed the inferno up close and personal, was something akin to a miracle.

There had been no trace of the artefact known as the Vase of Heaven. The small, humble-looking vase with a value in excess of eight million US dollars had not been recovered from the ashes of the destroyed warehouse. Kane couldn't help but feel remorse at his part in its destruction, but when he thought of Heung-min and that brave young man's traumatic ordeal, his terrible injuries and his near full recovery, given the options, Kane knew he would have made the exact same choice again.

Kane turned to look at the temple under a fading light as

the late afternoon drifted towards early evening. The reds, greens and blues of the ornately carved temple façade stood out like a beacon in the otherwise gloomy afternoon, and with a last glance at the carved Buddhist icons, mythical dragons and fierce warrior heads, Kane's mind turned to his close friend, Jae-won. Kane's former tae-kwon-do teacher had been more than a martial art's mentor to him. He had been a father figure, an inspiration, and a guru in all manner of life's facets. Kane had known many great men and women in his life, and Jae-won had been as pivotal as any of them over the course of the last two and a half decades since they'd first met on the tae-kwon-do mat way back when.

His heart ached at the loss he felt, yet he knew that somehow, Jae-won's love, compassion and indomitable spirit would remain with him always. As he stepped down the wooden stairs that led to the temple, Kane recalled something Jae-won had said to him just after he'd first arrived there at Golgulsa almost two months earlier. Kane had endured a series of nightmares involving the love of his life, Alexandria Ridley. Jae-won had seen and heard his friend's angst about his lost love, though Kane tried in vain to play it down. Jae-won had called him out about it.

"Call her," Jae-won had said one day when they'd been walking around the tomb park in downtown Gyeongju.

"Call who?" Kane had asked innocently. He hadn't realised then that he had fallen silent for the previous ten minutes, but Jae-won knew Kane well, better than he knew himself. When Kane was distant, as he was then, there was only one person he was thinking about.

Jae-won laughed. "You know who. Alexandria. Call Alex, my friend."

Kane had frowned at first, but then couldn't help the sheepish, knowing grin that spread across his face. "You got me," he'd said, offering Jae-won his trademark wry smile. "Can't hide anything from you, can I."

Jae-won shrugged, then said, "So will you call her? It will put *us* all out of *your* misery."

It had been a joke, but as Kane thought back on his friend's encouraging words now, Kane smiled again and vowed that once the dust had settled here, his next and only mission would be to track down and find the one person that he knew could complete his own recovery from his recent trials and tribulations.

At long last, Kane would find Alexandria Ridley.

More by Steven Moore

vinci-books.com/HiramKane

Follow the link to stay up to date with Steven Moore's new releases.

About the Author

Englishman Steven Moore grew up by the seaside, thus his first true joy was the great outdoors. His innate love of travel and a degree in anthropology, archaeology, and art history, help inform his fiction writing. Steven also loves painting, photography, and both playing and watching sport.

The travel bug bit the now perpetual nomad early, and to date Steven has lived and worked on five continents, and visited almost seventy countries. Steven combines an age-old writing adage; Write what you know, with his own mantra; Write where you know, and sets most of his novels in places in which he has either lived or spent an extended period of time.

When not on the road, Steven divides his time between Norwich, UK, and San Miguel de Allende, Mexico, which he shares with his rescue cats Ernest Hemingway and F Scott Fitzgerald (Ernie and Fitz), and his rescue puppy, Charles Dickens. Oh yes, and his beautiful travel writer wife, Leslie.

A lifelong love of food, wine, and beer, have demanded a new-found love of yoga and hiking in order to fend off the imminent arrival of middle age.

Acknowledgments

I don't know of any author who can finish a book of any kind without a lot of help and support, and I'm certainly no different. The assistance I've received for this novel and all my books has been both necessary and invaluable.

So, a quick shout out to these lovely folks—I couldn't have done it without you.

For the nuances of Korean culture, thanks, my friend 주혜박 (Ju-hye Park). Kam-sa hap-ni-da! 감사합니다

My gratitude to Anja Peerdeman, Michael Rhew and Tim Birmingham, my crucial BETA readers. Any remaining mistakes are my own. Thanks, guys.

I also want to thank the incredible team at Vinci Books for believing in me and supporting me on my journey. I appreciate you all.

And as always, to the one and only Leslie, my unstintingly supportive wife, I say thank you.

May you always be you!

Thank you! Kam-sa hap-ni-da! 감사합니다! (Hangul)

Steven